Razor Blade in Fun-Sized Candy

A Horror Comedy Anthology

Compiled and edited by Paul Lubaczewski

Razor Blade in Fun-Size Candy

A Horror Comedy Anthology

Compiled and Edited by Paul Lubaczewski

Published by St Rooster Books 2023

Cover by Stephanie and Tim Murr

This is a work of fiction. Any similarities between people alive or dead is coincidental, and possibly amusing.

Contact St Rooster Books at

Holyrooster76 @ Gmail dot com

Contents

For Jay Wilburn

Introduction

STOP! DON'T JUST SKIP THIS AND GO TO THE FIRST STORY!
THERE MIGHT BE INFORMATION IN HERE THAT COULD SAVE YOUR VERY LIFE!!!

Good, you're reading the introduction, so let's begin, shall we? Why horror comedy? It's a question I get asked all the time. I mean, not all the time. That would be pretty insane if it was all the time. Like if you were just getting your groceries and the butcher just blurted out, "Number 42! And oh yeah, by the way, why horror comedy?"

But I digress, if you've read my books, you would know that's a feature, not a defect. Being an author, I do a lot of interviews for the purpose of trying to convince the reading public to PLEASE DEAR GOD BUY MY BOOK! On almost every occasion the question does come up, along with how in the hell do I pronounce my name, (Dear interviewers, I am in no way suggesting that book tours are in any way repetitive or unpleasant at all. As far as I'm concerned you are all gods amongst men, and I bask in your reflective glory whenever I am interviewed by you, so please dear God have me back on soon.)

Well, anyway, now that I'm done sucking up. There are a few reasons why horror comedy, at least for me personally. Firstly, it's fun to read, that's why I do it, and hopefully why you read it. To give some background, I grew up in the perfect nexus to have the germs of the idea flow into my pointed little skull. The 70s in Philadelphia where I grew up was a golden age for horror. On Channel 48 you had Creature Double Feature, and over on 17, you had Shock Theater. We were literally that spoiled for choice that every Saturday afternoon we had three different horror films to choose from. (I know in the era of Shudder that doesn't seem much but trust me when you only have 6 channels and 2 of them are running horror flicks....)

At the same time, stand-up comedy was finally breaking big into the mainstream. George Carlin, Richard Pryor, and for the first time, a stand-up was filling out arenas on his own as Steve Martin's brand of absolute weirdness took the nation by storm.

On the movie front, two touchstone films came out. Young Frankenstein, and Love at First Bite. They might not have been the first films to deliver horror-comedy, but they were two of the first to deliver it smartly that were readily available instead of as slapstick setups.

Finally, as a teen, I discovered two authors who would set a new bar for what could be considered funny with the written word. Douglas Adams' "Hitchhiker's Guide to the Galaxy," and Terry Pratchett's Discworld series showed something else. Parody and humor were absolutely possible, at even Monty Python levels, no matter how stodgy and set in stone the genre might be. In fact, the stodgier the better. Horror comedy seemed the next logical evolution of the idea for me. Not just me, but for quite a few other authors. Horror is a genre rife with cliches, rife with unwritten rules, meant to be serious by its very nature. To a comedic mind, ripe for the picking.

It also makes sense in another way, and possibly the most logical one. How do humans deal with stress? We crack jokes. Humor is our outlet, a safe space where we can let go of our hardest emotions so that we can continue to deal with things. If anything, a horror novel with 0 sense of humor is unrealistic at its base. Gallows humor is the finest of human traditions, alright, not the finest, that's probably wiping after using the bathroom, but it's up there!

And despite all I've just written, horror-comedy is sort of the unappreciated red-headed stepchild of the publishing industry. It doesn't get awards, hell it doesn't get nominated, and we don't get invited onto NPR to talk in Ambien-induced whispers about the real meaning of our books. Bestselling authors like McCammon and King push us into lockers and give us wedgies, and then tell us we aren't allowed to even comment on whether that wedgie was funny or not.

It is neither easy to do nor is it an easy life. Which just gives us some more jokes to work into our stories. Thankfully the public still likes it, the books sell, and the films sell.

This comes to the reason for this book. I was recovering from knee surgery, and therefore heavily medicated. Also, I thought it would be fun and enjoyable to have an anthology that really highlighted the range the genre has and some of the talent there is working in it. I probably thought it would be fun because of all the medication, but once people start saying yes, they'll do it, you're kind of committed to it. I want to thank those people whose work you find here; they did a bang-up job of things. Also, thank the lord for St. Rooster for not saying, "New phone who dis?" when I proposed the idea.

Now here it is, and more or less exactly as I envisioned it in my drugged stupor. What I like about the anthology you're about to dig into is it does show the range of the genre, from full-out potty humor all the way to some slick and clever wordplay, from the bizarre to the parody, it's all in here. Which is a testament to the talent of the authors who didn't immediately block me on all social media when I started asking around for contributions.

Finally, I lied, there is no lifesaving information in this introduction, but I suckered you into reading it, so my work is done here.

-Paul Lubaczewski

What the Cat Dragged In

By: Nikki Nelson-Hicks

Outside the Double Wide:
C.W. Walker

"Fuck you, Doug."

C.W. Walker was having what his long-dead daddy would've called a "come to Jesus" moment. And he was hitting it hard.

"Fucking Doug."

C.W. threw the Budweiser at the crackling logs in his firepit and opened up another one.

He knew it would all come crashing down... eventually... but hell. Shit, how had it gone so wrong so fast?

A song from the 80s crooned out from the radio about lost youth, fighting against the wind, and asking the question, ... "twenty years...where did they go?"

"Fuck yeah, Bob, tell it." C.W. took a swallow and then poured out some on the ground as tribute. "I hear you, brother."

Twenty years? Hell, it was going on thirty, if he was honest. His half-century mark was only a few months away. How did he get so old so fast?

It wasn't supposed to be like this. *He* wasn't supposed to end up like this. What happened to his dream? He was supposed to be a race car driver by now. The next fucking Dale Earnhardt.

R.I.P. The Intimidator.

C.W. cast an eye at all the rusting junkers that littered his backyard. Broncos he spent weekends renovating until he spotted a sweet cherry red (except for the rusted parts) '81 Camaro that was crying out to be rehabbed into a passable Z-28. The Fords. The Chevys. Some of them only husks. Engines stashed in the garage. Some hanging from chains, like sides of metal beef. A few in parts, dissected, on tables, and others forgotten under tarps.

Christ. If he only had more time.

But time wasn't something C.W. had much to barter with ever since Douglas C. Wrightback came to town.

"Goddamn you, Doug."

He'd gotten his job at Thurston Motor Lines from a bad game of poker. He'd lost big but instead of taking an IOU, the Old Man held out his hand and said, "No problem, son. I've been there. You can work it off for me at my loading dock. Be there on Monday."

That was ten years ago. It was a sweet gig. Trucks would pull up, C.W. and the guys working day shift, Rooster, Teddy, and Eugene, would load them up. Day in, day out. The Old Man didn't give a damn about degrees or, best of all, DUIs. None of that mattered. If you had the strength to move shit around, you had a job. Those were the good days.

And then the Old Man upped and died.

Enter stage left, Douglas C. Wrightback, the Old Man's son-in-law, with his laptop and his goddamn Business Plan.

Overnight, C.W. and the crew needed special licenses to drive forklifts. Physical exams and drug tests became mandatory. High blood pressure and a tinge of cocaine could sideline you, sometimes permanently. And a single DUI? Forget about it. Pack up your shit and go home.

But the thing that finally broke the camel's back was the Education Program. Everyone on the dock was forced to show proof of their high school diploma. And if you didn't have one, all employees were required to get a GED. On your own dime, no less.

A goddamn piece of paper to push pallets around.

"Fuck you, Doug."

C.W. threw a half-full bottle of Bud at the fire. He'd expected a whoosh and crash, like in the movies, but the flame just fizzled and made sad popping noises.

"Story of my goddamn life," he muttered.

A voice screeched out at him through the screen door. "C.W.! You sorry son of a bitch!"

And here comes the icing on my bitch cake. He turned to see his wife of too many damn years, Julene, screaming at him from the back door. She had on her witchy robe. *Aw, Christ. That's not good.*

Back in the day, he thought banging a crazy goth chick would be hot. And it was, for a while but, eventually, it just gets creepy. Three years into this freak show and the whole damn house looked like something from a Halloween Express. Skulls, candles, stuffed bats, and dozens of jars covered in wax that he learned the hard way to never ask about.

It didn't stop there. Hell, no. Her divine ya-ya-hood had flowed outside the realm of the double-wide to the backyard. HIS goddamn backyard! That got up his butt. The back should be a man's domain. It's where C.W. could take apart a V-8 engine in peace. Him and the boys could gather around the fire pit, drink, smoke weed, and talk shit. Those were the fucking days.

Now, there were Tibetan Prayer flags in all the colors of the rainbow along with a dozen wind chimes that rattled off key. She dug up patches of his lawn to start up herb gardens from "sacred seeds" sanctified by a coven and a "serenity corner, with a plastic koi pond held up by 72 cinder blocks imported from Solana Beach, California because she couldn't do with the ones down at the local Home Depot. Oh, no, blessed cinder blocks packed with special red dirt blessed by some goddamn hippy in Sedona. Next came the fish. Nine slippery, foreign bastards. "Because the number nine is lucky in Feng Shui," she explained, and then she'd go on and on and on about the colors and symbolism. Ogon, Kikokuryu, Kukaku, Bukaki, or something or other. He stopped listening. Hell, she could have been naming Pokémon for all C.W. cared. The only thing that mattered was now there was a goddamn kidney-shaped plastic tub, filled with too many foreign, terrorist fish, taking up valuable space where his race car used to be.

Ain't no place for a man to hang with his boys. Hell, no. This rainbow shit would get him beat up for sure.

"C.W.! Are you listening to me?"

"What the hell do you want?"

"Where is my uise beatha?" said Julene.

"Ishka ba what? I don't know what the fuck you're talking about!"

"My ceremonial whiskey, you drunk fuck. It's

gone."

"I ain't got your goddamn whiskey, woman!"

"If I find out you're lying to me if I smell just a whiff of whiskey on your breath," she made a snapping sound with her tongue. "You're next on my hex list. And don't you scratch up my Seger CD!"

"Whatever, woman." C.W. slid back down in his chair. He opened up another bottle, the froth splashing on his vintage Lynyrd Skynyrd concert shirt. "Goddammit. Why can't I have anything nice?"

At his feet, the prophet in the boombox screamed out: *I stood tall and I stood strong...I still believed in my dreams.*

Damn, but Seger hit harder the older a man got. He remembered back in the day when he'd throw back his head, screaming into the night, singing about running against the wind, feeling strong, having all the time in the world at his feet. God, those were the days. Free and young.

Now, that song put a hot stone in C.W. Walker's gut. *Easy for that fucker to say. Probably sitting in a marble mansion somewhere in Beverly Hills. What the fuck would he know about sitting in the backyard, surrounded by dead plants, a pool of stinking fish, and staring at the rusted carcasses of what should have been?*

"Fuck you, Doug." C.W. threw his last bottle in the fire. "And fuck you too, Bob, wherever you are."

C.W. let himself sink down in his chair. No beer. A fire that was dying at his feet. He let himself fall deeper and deeper into that dark hole that pulled him down, down, down.

Fuck this, fuck that and-

Suddenly, a scream, high and shrill, from behind his junk heap of rusting cars, cut through the night.

"What the fuck?"

From underneath the car, Booper, an old gray alley cat with torn ears and a tail that was bent at the tip, that roamed his graveyard of cars, crawled out from under a Chevy with something bleeding and writhing in his snaggle-toothed maw.

"Whatcha' got there, Boop? Another rat?"

C.W. had only a second before a whoosh of gray fur and scraping sharp claws used the old man as a jumping board and then dashed under the double-wide trailer.

"OW, Jesus fuck, Boop! What the hell?"

The thing in Booper's mouth twisted around and looked C.W. in the eyes.

C.W. squinted. "What the hell did you catch, Boop?"

The thing in the cat's mouth, shrieked, releasing a tsunami of sound.

"Fuck!" C.W. screamed and fell to his knees, as the sound tore through his body, shaking his guts so hard that his intestines rolled and exploded. Behind him, the glass wind chimes shattered, and the metal rods melted off their strings.

The cat growled and went deeper into the shadows of the double wide.

Panting, C.W. Walker felt the wetness on the back of his jeans, sniffed the shit on his fingertips, and stared at the darkness under the double wide.

Bright green eyes blinked back.

Inside the Double Wide:
Julene Walker

Julene took a long draw from her cigarette and slowly exhaled, blowing the white smoke into the empty jar until it rolled out over the rim like storm clouds.

"So, mote it fucking be," she said, putting the jar aside.

She assembled everything she needed to put that bitch Dory Tey in her place: white fabric, a photograph, red and black thread, some of the bitch's hair that Gloria at the beauty salon swept up for her, broken shards of glass, barbed wire, urine, black candles and a few extra herbs to really give the spell a kick.

First, she cut out a poppet from white muslin and placed it inside a photo of Dory that she swiped off Facebook. It was one of those drunken "Look at me and my man!" selfies that made Julene hate her even more. Who the hell did she think she was? Did she really think she could do what the girls said she did, say what the girls said she said, and get away with it? Aw to the hell naw. This little slut needed to learn what happens when you fuck with the biggest, baddest witch in town.

She slowly sewed the doll shut with black thread, repeating the words, "With this needle, I stab you. With this thread, I bind you" with each stitch. She made Xs for eyes with the red thread. No mouth was needed since Julene wanted to silence the bitch, after all.

When the doll was finished, she stuffed it painfully into the small jar.

Then she took an eye dropper and sprinkled a few drops of her urine on the doll. "I excrete you like old water."

She dropped in the dishwater blonde hair. "Hair, to bind you."

Julene carefully picked up the shards of broken glass and put them inside the jar. "Glass to cut you."

Next came her favorite part, the herbs. First, jimson weed that grew wild in the field behind her house. "To poison and drive insane any plans."

Chili pepper. "To spread discord and irritation."

Stinging nettles. "For bad luck."

Poppy seed from her spice rack. "For marital discord."

And then she spit in it, just for fun.

She screwed the lid on tight, biting her lower lip in the effort. Then she wrapped the entire jar in barbed wire, careful not to cut herself and spill any of her blood, and covered the jar in black candle wax. Now is when she'd seal the deal by pouring uise beatha over the jar as an offering to spirits, but plain old Jack Daniels would do in a pinch.

Smiling at a job well done, Julene carefully picked up the jar and placed it on the windowsill above the sink with all the others.

She had the best collection of hex jars in the county.

Among her favorites was Tammie Wilton, who owned a New Age shop in the next county over who thought she was all that because she hosted the yearly Cosmic Psychic Convention. Last year, she wouldn't allow Julene to rent a booth because

Tammie said that her vulva-shaped pastries were pornographic and inappropriate. The old prude nearly fell over when she caught sight of a batch of Julene's Dicker Doodles.

Julene hoped she enjoyed that yearlong UTI.

And then there was Charles Jackson, the manager at the Piggly Wiggly, who wouldn't allow her to cash a two-party check even though he knew damn well that she was, more than not, good for it.

She was sad to see the Piggly Wiggly burn down but, that's the breaks.

And now there was this new bitch in town, Dory Tey. Little miss prissy with the long blonde hair, high and tight tits, and the ass that won't quit. This bitch. This *bitch* thinks she can bring her Southern California crystals and candles and stand up to some old Appalachian witchy work? Come into my town, push through my wards, and try to take my throne?

Julene felt the crackling of power rush through her veins and pulse out her fingertips. She focused the rage and tapped Dory Tey's jar with one fingertip.

The thick black wax cracked into a line of spiderwebs.

"Fuck around and find out, *hon.*"

It was hard work, but a witch has to do what a witch has to do.

There was a pounding at the back door.

It was C.W.

"WOMAN!"

Julene rolled her eyes. The man was a goddamn idiot, but his paychecks kept the wolf away from the door and her off of welfare.

"What?"

"Open the....get off me, you damn cat!....open the goddamn door....ugh! Get the fuck off me, cat!"

"Hold your goddamn horses," she said and flipped the deadbolt.

C.W. rushed in, holding a bundle close to his chest.

Mr. Booper was desperately climbing up C.W. like a tree.

"Get that goddamn cat! Off me! OFF!" C.W. screamed and shook his leg but the cat held firm.

"Jesus, C.W.! Did you shit yourself?"

"One thing at a time, Woman. First, get this damn cat!"

Mr. Booper howled as Julene untangled the cat from C.W.'s soiled jeans.

"What the hell has got into him?"

"This." C.W. patted the lump he had rolled up in the end of his vintage t-shirt. "Look at what the cat caught."

He leaned over the kitchen table, unfolded his shirt, and a...*thing* rolled out.

It was little more than ten inches. It looked like melted caramel, curled up like a gooey fetus so it was hard to tell which end was what. From its back, there were two sharp, bat-like wings. One laid down flat while the other jutted up, obviously broken by Booper's attack. C.W. poked at it with his finger. There was a guttural sigh as the thing deflated and unrolled itself, flattening out like a grotesque blobfish. From this position, two ends of the thing could be made out: one ended in two clawed feet like a chicken and the other a gaping mouth lined with tiny, sharp teeth.

Two slits above the mouth were closed tightly as if the thing were in agonizing pain.

C.W. leered over his prize. "What do you think it is?"

Julene dropped the cat on the floor. "Oh, honey, I know exactly what that is."

She lit a cigarette, took a long draw, and blew the white smoke into the face of the thing. Four tiny arms emerged from its chest and waved the smoke away with beautifully, delicate hands like from a porcelain doll.

C.W. jumped back. "What the fuck?!?"

"Ha! If that bitch, Dory Tey, thinks sending a goddamn elemental to do her dirty work is going to play in my house, HA! Oh, she is in for something now!" Julene stomped over to the cabinet and pulled out a large mason jar. The glass was thick, tinted green, and etched with symbols. She opened it and shook out some remaining salt that clung to the sides.

"This will do. Hand me that spatula."

C.W. did as he was told and watched in fascinated revulsion as Julene used it to scoop the freakish thing into the jar. As it slid down the glass, it groaned and shrieked.

"Oh, shut up!" She screwed the lid on tightly and shook it violently. "Reveal yourself!" she commanded. "Show your true form, fucker!"

The thing inside twisted painfully, like salt taffy going through a wringer, until it congealed into a solid shape. It no longer looked like a blob of congealed jam. It was solid, smooth, and the color of bronze with a sculpted torso, chicken-like legs, and stubby arms of a small monkey. It had two feathered wings, one lying flat on its back while the other one jutted upwards at an obscene angle. The head was a confusing mixture of dragon and hawk, with scales and feathers intertwined, a snout like a crocodile, and the sharp, heavy-lidded eyes of a raptor.

It stared into Julene with absolute, fiery hatred.

"Aw, don't start up with that shit!" she said, shaking the jar like it was a marimba. She set the jar on the table and stood at her full height of 5' 4" and that included her jet-black honeycomb of a do and looked down imperiously. "I know you, demon. I name you-"

"MEWOWRRRR!" Mr. Booper lept up to the table and swiped at the jar. Its claws scratched against the glass and the thing inside the jar cowered and bowed.

"Jesus!" C.W. caught the jar before it fell off the table. "Get that damn cat!"

"Goddamnit, Mr. Booper!" Julene grabbed the hissing and snarling cat by the scruff of its neck. "OOF! You weigh a ton! C.W., you told me you got this damn cat neutered."

"Those do-gooders down at the pound did it, not me. Remember last summer, they came 'round and caught all the feral toms out back. Look, they even notched his ear!"

"Sure they did. And his balls just grew back naturally."

Julene dropped the cat outside. It hit the ground, turned, and ran straight for the closest window.

Mr. Booper sat on the window ledge, his tail twitching.

"Now, back to where I was," said Julene,

patting her hair and clearing her throat. "I name you, Demon, Elemental-"

The creature smiled with a mouth of a thousand sharp stinging teeth and started giggling. The sound resonated like sharp nails on a chalkboard.

C.W. grabbed his ears and clenched his ass tight.

"Demon? Elemental? That's a terrible insult to a high born of the Smokeless Flame, Julene." The creature's golden fiery eyes flared up at the naming of the woman.

"Fuck." Julene's rouge looked like red gashes on her pale cheeks. "Well, I'll be damned."

Crossing one taloned foot over its leg in a figure four, it leaned back, crunching its broken wing against the jar. It began to pick its teeth with a talon, pulling out a blob of meat, and swallowing it.

"What? What is it, Julene?"

Julene smacked her lips and put a hand on her gracious hip. "It looks like the cat dragged in a goddamn Djinn."

A deep musical laughter echoed from inside the jar. "Nicely guessed, hag. Now, set me free so I can grant the wishes of my captor."

"Did it say wishes?" asked C.W. "Is that thing a genie? Like that dude that comes out of a bottle and grants wishes?"

"You really are a low vibrating motherfucker, C.W." Julene took a deep drag off her cigarette, exhaled, and shook her head. "They can do more than just wishes. Other than Angels, Djinn are the most powerful celestial beings out there."

"Huh, if it's so powerful, how come it's stuck

inside a mason jar?"

"Perhaps it amuses me," answered the Djinn.

A brutal smile crossed Julene's face. "Oh, that's not true, is it? You can't get out because it's sealed."

"So, why don't it just unscrew the top."

"Not the lid, you fucking moron. The seal!" She pointed at the embossed marking. "See, back in the day, King Solomon found a way to enslave Djinns with this sigil." She tapped it with a long red fingernail. "Forced your people to build the temple in Jerusalem, if memory serves. After Solomon's death, the enslaved Djinn were freed but they can still be caught and bound by anyone using the mark. That's why it's stuck inside my jar."

"Hell's bells, Julene! What are we waiting for?" C.W. snatched the jar from the table. "I know exactly what I want to wish for."

"Stop! Don't say another word, C.W.!" Julene wrestled the jar from her husband's tight grip. "Now, listen to me. It ain't like in Aladdin, okay? This thing does not want to be your best friend. Hell, they hate us humans. These motherfuckers are tricksters. Whatever we wish for, it'll find a way to screw us in the ass. Don't you watch Twilight Zone?"

"But...Julene ..."

"No, I...we gotta think this through, babe." She pulled him closer and gave him a bright smile, the kind she used to give back in the day when she could still stand the idea of him touching her; she could feel him start to melt. She lifted her voice an octave higher. *The baby voice always wins.* "Trust me, babe. We need to take this slow."

"But, Julene..."

"Babe, don't you trust me?"

C.W. sighed. "Yeah. I guess so."

Julene patted his shoulder.

"Good. Now, go take a shower. Do you want to start our new lives with a load of shit in your drawers?"

C.W.'s shoulders slumped as he grunted, "'kay."

She watched her husband drag his feet down the hall like a frustrated kid on Christmas Eve.

Idiot.

She lifted the jar to her eye level and stared into the Djinn's burning eyes until it blinked.

She kissed the jar, leaving behind a stain of purple lips, placed it gently on the kitchen table, and patted the lid like a pet dog.

"Oh, the fun we're going to have. Things are sure as hell going to change around here."

She turned off the lights, leaving only the smoldering eyes of the Djinn to shine in the dingy darkness.

Outside the Double Wide:
Mr. Booper

Small, sharp claws plucked the metal window screen like a guitar.

Pluck.

Pluck.

BOING.

Pluck.

Pluck.

BING.

A satisfied growl burbled up from the old cat's throat as the tear in the screen grew larger.

There were dozens of feral cats that lived in the junk heaps behind the Walker double-wide. At one time, so the elder cats say, their ancestors roamed the land in the times before Man like a furry fog of claws and teeth. Prey was plentiful. Birds, squirrels, and rats all bowed their heads to the great hordes. There were trees and green places to hunt, prey, and play. It was a blessed, ferocious time, lost when humans came in like a plague of ticks, tore down the forests, mowed down the fields, and, worst of all, brought with them filthy packs of dogs.

Paths were flattened and covered in hard black rock where murderous metal monsters roared past, crushing anything too slow to make it across in time.

Then came the Takings.

Toms would be captured in cages, taken away, and returned but with only a notch in their ears to tell the tale. Now, the clowder was only a handful left of sullen Mollies and fat, lazy Toms.

Those ferocious days lived only in the tales told to kittens as they nursed on their mothers.

Back when there were kittens...

None of the Mollies have spawned a litter in seasons.

It is a disgrace, how our pride is taken from us, the old tom mused. *But our time will come again.*

A few more plucks and it was large enough for the old tom's head. His whiskers plastered back as he pushed his grizzled face through the torn screen and, soon, the rest of the cat followed behind.

The cat hopped down from the window and padded its way across the linoleum. Once it reached the table, it took a moment or two to gauge the right amount of force it would take to reach the top; it had been a long time since it had such a full belly. The cat wriggled its haunches, enjoying the sway of the newly restored testicles, and leapt, gravity seemingly ignoring the hefty cat, as it landed solidly on the table.

Its prize lay ahead.

"Meowrrrr?" It pawed the jar, pushing it slightly.

The prize inside lifted its head and stared intently into the cat's eyes.

Hail, Grimalkin. Come to finish our deal? What do you desire?

The cat nudged the jar with a clawed mitt in frustration. "Grrrrpfffft!"

A wonderful wish! Wise and very, very practical. So be it! With all my powers, so it shall be. You and I share common enemies, Grimalkin. By the Sacraments and Celestial Laws, I will have vengeance. By all that is holy in this godforsaken hellspace, I vow! All you must do now is free me.

The edge of the table crept closer with each swipe. The Djinn lowered its head in submission, pulled its knees to his chest, and hugged its tattered wings tightly around its body.

Inshallah.

Inside the Double-Wide:
C.W. Walker

C.W. slammed the door and cursed under his breath, "Fuck! Fuck! Fuck that bitch!"

The bathroom was barely big enough to swing a cat. A toilet, a sink, and a shower. Hell, he'd seen better setups in truck stops back when he used to drive 18-wheelers across the country. He leaned against the sink and stared at the old man who looked back at him in the mirror.

"This ain't how it should be," he says to the old man. "We got everything we need to make it out of here. But she wants to wait!"

The old man in the mirror smiled back at C.W.

"Why should I wait for her?"

A plan was forming. Oh, yes.

"But first..."

He kicked off his knock-off Adidas into the corner, pulled off the old concert t-shirt, socks, and jeans, balled them tightly, and tossed it like he was dunking a winning game ball into the hamper.

But the underwear. There was no saving that.

His shit had congealed into a thick brown paste that glued his whitey tighties to his butt cheeks. He slowly peeled his BVDs off his ass and gagged as he dropped the whole sticky mess to his feet, hop skipping out, nearly falling down in the effort.

He turned on the shower, waited for the water to heat up, and kicked the shit-stained undies to the corner, next to the small trash can by the door. Close enough.

A three-tiered plastic rack hung off the showerhead with all of Julene's toiletries. She had three different creams, soaps, and assorted fruity-smelling body lotions for every crook and cranny. Not that he'd had the pleasure of any of those bits in years.

C.W. had a bar of antibacterial soap and two-in-one shampoo/conditioner that he kept in the corner of the stall. What else did a person need?

He stood with his back to the spray, holding his butt cheeks apart so the water could jet blast most of the funk off his backside. He grabbed the bar of soap, rubbed it until it became a frothy mess, and spread that antibacterial goodness all over his body, taking special care around his Crown Jewels and Brown Eyed Sally. Then his pits and chest. He turned and let the hot water rush over his face. He reached blindly behind him, grabbed the shampoo/conditioner, squirted out a half-dollar-sized dollop into his hand, and slapped it on top of his head. He vigorously scrubbed his scalp until the soapy bubbles rolled down the rest of his body. All in all, his ablutions took about five minutes.

He stood there, hot water blasting over his face, feeling clean, a tad bit more sober, and thought about what he would do with all the power of a wish.

He got three wishes if the movies were right. Three chances to make his life a fuck load better.

Number one: Fuck that fucker Doug Wrightback. Have him disappear and make C.W.

Walker the CEO and Big Boss Man of Thurston Motor Lines.

Number two: Shave off ten...no, twenty years. He rubbed his hand over his thick beer belly. Turn back the clock to when he was young, vital, and hard as a rock.

Number three: All the pussy he could handle. Good pussy, too. Young and wet, a bunch of bitches who wanted to ride him all day and night. A harem that wanted nothing else in life but to dip his wick deep inside their thighs, balls and all.

He felt a deep satisfaction as he ripped a cleansing fart and imagined a world where C.W. Walker was King of all that he surveyed.

The only thing he needed to do was get his hands on that fucking jar before Julene.

Inside the Double Wide:
Julene Walker

Julene Walker sat down at her pink and white vanity table and stared into the ornate mirror hanging on the wall.

Mirror, mirror on the wall. Who is the baddest witch of all?

She didn't wait for an answer. She didn't need one. The one thing she had over that stupid bitch in the fairy tales is that she didn't need anyone to stroke her ego. She knew the answer. Who's the baddest witch? I am... because I fucking said so.

Still, having a Djinn on her side would give her a nice boost in the street cred department.

Julene didn't believe in the limit of three wishes. Why should there be a limit? As long as she held all the cards, she had all the power. She figured if she kept it imprisoned like Solomon had done, wishes were unlimited. She was the boss. She could have eternal youth! Unlimited wealth! The best parking spot at Wal-Mart!

All that power. ALL of it mine to control.

As she ruminated on that thought, a red-hot tingle blossomed in her root chakra and rippled up her spine causing her to gasp loudly. "Power!" she cried out as she orgasmed, her fingernails scratching the pink satin chair cushions.

The balloon of her reverie was burst by the sound of a loud fart coming from the shower.

First things first, that son of a bitch has got to go.

Inside the Double Wide:
A Room of Compromise

The bedroom of C.W. and Julene Walker was a room of compromise.

In the sense that she had her side and he learned to be happy with what was left over.

In the 144 square feet that encompassed the room, Julene claimed the closet, three drawers of the dresser, ¾ of the floor space that included a meditation station, a Pilates mat, and the vanity table.

C.W. had one dresser drawer, a nightstand, and roughly 8 inches of the queen-sized mattress to call his own.

Tonight, they laid in bed, their backsides to each other, and pretended to sleep.

Neither of them trusted the other enough to close their eyes for a second.

Julene knew that bastard was up to no good when he came to bed wearing a shirt and boxers when he normally slept in the raw. While she was thankful not to see his hairy flanks scuffing up her new sateen sheets, she saw it for what it was: he was planning something, and it didn't take a crystal ball to figure out what.

Julene stared into the darkness, fingering her pillowcase and wondering if her goose-down pillow was heavy enough to smother the old fart.

C.W. stared at the closed bedroom door, his brain ruminating on what his wife was planning. When was the last time she went to bed without putting her hair up in rollers and slathering royal jelly lotion on her face? "Oh, I was just too tired tonight," she said, yawning.

C.W. called bullshit. She's going to hit the floor running the second he fell asleep.

He eyed his leather belt laying on the floor, inches away. He imagined looping it around her throat and throttling her until her eyes rolled back and then, lights out, baby.

He chuckled.

"What?" said Julene. "Did you say something?"

"Um…no, just-"

He was interrupted by the sound of glass crashing, laughter, and a giant boom of thunder coming from the kitchen.

They both sat up, looked at each other for a millisecond before scrambling and pushing against the other to be the first out of the door.

Inside the Double Wide:
The Final Wish

C.W. and Julene Walker ran down the short hallway, pushing and clawing at each other until they both came to a dead stop.

Ahead of them was a wasteland of destruction. The living room, kitchenette, and kitchen were torn apart as if a cyclone had been let loose in the double-wide. The rattan coffee table had been shredded into wheat thins. The couch cushions had been ripped and the foam matting burst through the fabric like moldy dough. The kitchen table had been thrown with such force that the legs were embedded in the ceiling. The altars to Shakti, Hecate, and to the Morrigan were flattened as if stepped on by an invisible elephant. All the herbs, containers, and spell books on the kitchen counter were tossed onto the floor and covered in something wet and foul-smelling.

As they stepped closer to the destruction, it was that smell that made them both take a step back into the hallway. C.W. squeezed his nose shut with his Guns and Roses t-shirt. Julene held a hand up to her mouth to keep from vomiting.

"Where is it?" C.W. said, his voice quacking like a duck.

As a response, the open jar, broken around the rim but still very much intact, rolled up to their feet.

"Oh shit."

"Out of my way, idiot." Julene pushed her husband aside and peeked into the kitchen.

The Djinn had its back to her and was

floating three feet off the floor. It was no longer the twisted monkey thing with the broken wing that hunkered inside the mason jar. It was glorious. It was now so tall that its head scraped the ceiling. A long purple cloak with pulsating golden embellishments that ran through the fabric like a network of throbbing veins draped over its broad, muscular shoulders and swept across the floor. There were three sets of black feathered wings, flapping lazily. One of them still had a bent in the tip from the former break. Luscious golden hair flowed around its head like a burning halo. The Djinn was humming a strange tune in three different octaves as it flicked Julene's hex jars off the windowsill.

"Hey! Stop that!" Julene rushed towards the Djinn. "I command you to stop!"

The Djinn's long tapered claw stopped beside the second to last hex jar. It looked over its shoulder at the tiny woman. Where eyes should be were six dark holes with a spark of red and gold fire flaming within. It arched several eyebrows and smiled with a mouth that held a thousand sharpened teeth.

It flicked the hex jar to the floor. A whiff of sulfur and a bang of light popped as the bottle smashed on the floor.

Julene screamed in frustration. "I am your master! I held you captive. By lore, you must obey me!"

A deep, dark laugh that sounded as if it came from a hundred throats erupted from the Djinn, breaking the remaining windows and shaking the house to its foundation.

C.W. cowered behind his wife and grabbed

her arm. "Julene, let it go. Okay? We gotta get outta' here…"

"Let go, you old fart! I'm not giving up. Not when I'm so close!" Julene pulled her arm away, reached down, and picked up the broken mason jar. "Do you remember this? The Seal of Solomon? Ah, I can see you remember that, don't you?"

"Oh, yes. I shall always remember your inhospitality and discourteousness, you vile abomination of dirt, but you are not the one to whom I was beholden. There are rules, you stupid slug. There is a matter of honor that lends itself to the price of my allegiance. You did not best me in battle, hag. Truth be told, I was settling up the wages of battle with my true Conqueror when your fool consort scooped me up in his soiled undershirt as if I were nothing but cabbage. There was no honor in that, NO! I owe you nothing, harridan."

The Djinn bowed to the shadows.

"Are you satisfied, my Master? I have provided all that you commanded. A full belly, the reconstitution of your virility, but, before we finish our arrangement, may I ask for one favor? Pray, honorable sire, to permit me the pleasure of witnessing the domination of your enemies."

A loud, rolling purr answered him.

The Djinn smiled as he nodded, "You are as gracious as you are powerful. Many thanks!"

"What the hell is he talking about, Julene? Ain't nobody here but us."

A low growl undulated from the shadows that seemed to thicken all around them. The sound of thick claws clacking on the linoleum followed as a giant cat, a nightmare from the primordial past, the collection of genetic memories that live in the dreams of all house cats, from tabbies to calicos, the Big Cat, the hunter, the devourer, the death that came with fangs and claws, emerged from the darkness.

Julene's eyes widened in deadly realization. "Mr. Booper?"

The cat that once answered to the indignant name of Mr. Booper yawned in response, his mouth gaping widely to show off each and every knife-edged, spikey fang and molar. He lowered his gaze, his burning golden eyes glared at his prey and a rough-coated tongue licked clean his slavering, grey-muzzled maw.

"Wait," asked C.W. "Are you telling me....the fucking cat?"

And then the nightmare cat leapt.

C.W. Walker crunched under the nightmare cat's thick paws. With a quick swipe, the man's gullet ripped out with velvety ease. The cat licked at the fountain of blood as it sprayed out until the little man beneath him stopped wriggling.

Bored, it turned towards the squirming woman.

"No...no...please.... Mr. Booper..." Julene backed away slowly until she tripped over the destroyed coffee table. She looked over to the Djinn who was leaning casually against the sink. "Help me! Please! I'll give you any-"

The nightmare cat engulfed her head and popped it off with one sharp turn of its head.

The Djinn tipped the final hex jar, satisfied.

Inshallah.
THE END

Pubes

By: R.J. Benetti

They called it trichotillomania, or trich, for short. In unscientific terms, it was the unstoppable urge to pluck out your own hair, usually by the root.

Danny's slim, finicky mother, Annabelle, suspected he had it bad. And that's how he found himself where he was today. In the bright doctor's office, with dread dripping from every pore.

"How unusual," said the dermatologist, Dr. Willard Keats, a balding, heavyset man with a pencil-thin mustache and thick, black spectacles. "The boy has a full head of hair. He doesn't seem to be pulling out anything at all."

Annabelle began to wallow. "It's his ot-other hair. His..." She pointed at her son's pelvic region, her finger trembling. "His pubic hair!"

"Erm... His pu-pubic hair? Is this true, boy?"

Danny rocked in his seat. "You don't understand. I have to," he said, his voice quivering. "The fate of the world depends on it."

Dr. Keats traced his eyes down Danny's arms, so he could take a look at the boy's hands. He noticed that they were completely obscured under the elastic waistband of his basketball shorts, and they were doing... *something*, fidgeting beneath the fabric, jerking up and down with sharp movements.

"Unhand yourself!" squawked the doctor.

"Cut it out, Danny! We're in the doctor's office!" screamed Annabelle.

Shaking his head, Danny sprung from the plastic seat and made his way to the door. The doctor was on him in a moment, grabbing him by the shoulders and turning him around.

"Please, son. Cut this out. You're worrying your kind mother."

"I CAN'T!" Danny yelled.

Dr. Keats' lips thinned, which looked strange beneath his thin mustache, like two parallel lines, yet opposites—one line white, the other black. Sighing, he patted the teen's shoulders, deciding to employ some tact.

"Everything's going to be fine. Just drop your trousers and we'll see what all this fuss is about."

Danny shot a glance at his mother, his eyes growing big and scared. She nodded, stifling some cries in her throat, pressing a crumpled-up tissue to her mousy, pink nose.

"Just do as the doctor says, Danny. He can help you. Please, show him."

Looking down with a swiftness, then back up with a movement just as quick, Danny narrowed his gaze on the doctor.

"You don't want to see this. I'm not crazy! I'm telling you; the fate of the world depends on me not having pubes!"

Like a clown on laughing gas, Keats chuckled, and said, "Son, I've been in this profession for over forty years. There's nothing I haven't seen before, and I can assure you, that your—*ahem*—puberty and growth of pubic hair will not stop this 4.6-billion-year-old earth from spinning. Let's see what we're dealing with here."

Keats fiddled with his glasses, his waiting eyes resembling raisins behind his thick lenses.

Swallowing dryly, glancing once more at his mother for reassurance, Danny nodded, in a resigned sort of way, sighed, and pulled his basketball shorts down to his bony knees.

The Doctor fell back on his big ass. "What the *FUCK IS THAT!?*" he screamed, crab-walking backward.

For Danny's pubes were mostly gone, yanked out from their pores to leave little bloody scabs behind, making the visible swaths of flesh resemble irritated goose skin.

The pubes that did remain, made a strange, geometrical symbol, almost like a crop circle, except instead of corn it was composed of short and curlies.

The symbol was one that Danny had no clue he was making, he honestly tried to eradicate all of his short hairs, but the different patterns kept showing up, and with them came the fear.

That sinking pit of despair that tore down his esophagus and exploded in his heart, that *knowledge* that yes, he had definitely been abducted by aliens once, and yes, they had definitely probed him with many different-sized accouterments, and yes, they had done something to him so that his pubes were a threat to mankind.

What does this mean!? Danny wondered, tearfully looking at the zigzagging swirl with a little boxy critter walking like an Egyptian up top and then the circles, some filled in, and others not.

"JESUS, MADONNA, AND JEBEDIAH," Annabelle blessed herself, her hand moving in confused orbits, hovering over regions of her body while making little, separate, tiny crosses.

Danny hiked up his pants. "I told you, Mom!"

Composing himself, Dr. Keats began lifting his shaky, big frame up with the support of his desk.

"Sorry, just never seen something so danged *evil*-looking before. Scared the bing-bongs out of me, just had a visceral reaction. You have some artistic skill, son, you just have to stop taking it out on your genitals."

Danny looked around, his focus like a spotlight that settled on his mother, then went back to the doctor, then back again.

He remembered the faces of the aliens. Grey, with black, glossy eyes the shape and size of humongonoid almonds, and tiny mouths, about the circumference of a dime.

And he remembered... something like noodles writhing under their grey flesh.

Bobbling his head, as fright worked its chilly fingers into his vertebrae, Danny rushed past the doctor, shoulder-checking him so that he keeled back to the floor, then he banged into his skinny mother, sending her crashing against a wall with a "BE A PELICAN, NOT A PELI-CAN'T" motivational poster that brandished an image of a glossy pelican staring at a setting sun.

Danny leapt over her thin, semiconscious body, shattering his way through the office's window, plummeting to the grass below.

Luckily, there was a big, prickly bush there to catch him.

It reminded him of pubes.

* * *

Danny could feel his pubic hair growing, slithering from their pores like skinny serpents coming out of hiding.

"No! No! No!"

With sweat wetting his sideburns, he gritted his teeth at the bus stop, sitting on the concrete bench under the plexiglass diorama thing.

A crusty, bearded homeless man looked over, shivered, and screwed up his face, then slid further down the bench, busying his eyes with a streetlamp, even though it'd long burned out.

"Got ya bitch!"

Danny pinched, HARD, trapping a very small pube between his thumb and forefinger. His eyes welled with tears, and his cheeks flushed a fire engine red.

"Yaaaaaaaah!" he screamed, wrenching his pelvis with such power he lifted himself to his feet, his hips jerking forward.

"Fucking white people," muttered the homeless man, rising on shaky knees to quickly shamble away.

"Got ya! Got ya! Got ya!"

Danny plucked and plucked at his pubes. It was like a Whac-a-Mole game, one that made his nostrils flare, one that made him go *achoo!* involuntarily.

As he ripped his pubes from their roots, he spotted a white van coming around the corner. It turned at such a velocity that it hunkered down on one side, the wheels on the other almost lifting from the asphalt.

Its tires spun 'round, screeching like rubber banshees as Danny backpedaled and turned away. He heard the doors slide open behind him, banging into their hinges while the sound of boots slapped over the pavement.

He began running, tugging at his pubes and whimpering as he went, which slowed him down considerably, since he was kind of hobbling.

They gained on him fast, so, for a moment, he stopped prying the hairs from his scrotum and made way for a tall, chain-link fence.

Climbing was surprisingly easy, due to the abnormal strength pube-plucking had bestowed on his forearms, and, before he knew it, he straddled the tall fence, looking down at the men below.

"Come with us, we're here to help you!" shouted one of the white-clothed individuals.

A helicopter whirred its blades overhead, shining a light down that brought the dark, damp area to a state of brief brilliance.

"I'm doing this for you!" yelled Danny, watching the faces of the strangers as they began to climb, glowing and flashing, turning briefly into the bulbous, off-putting countenances of the aliens who'd abducted him.

"Ahhhhhh!" Danny fell, his body smacking down a steep concrete escarpment, rolling to the creek below.

***

Washing through the green-brown sludge of the sewers, with his head disappearing then reappearing under the tide of poop and refuse, Danny swam.

Well, swam as best as he could, because he was still plucking at his pubes, even underwater, even enshrouded in the dark with foul, fragrant fluid seeping into his every opening.

Just keep pulling the pubes... Just keep pulling them, he thought, seeing a fire up ahead, burning in a metal barrel, casting a coral glow through the length of the sewer.

A bunch of ratty, haggard individuals gathered around said barrel. For some unconscious reason, as he drifted forth, he clenched his butt cheeks.

***

"Name's Lazlo," said a homeless man wearing about thirteen coats, with patches of beard scraggle riddling his smudged face, a threadbare beanie on his head, and earmuffs concealing his listeners.

"That there's Jerry the Small," Lazlo pointed to another man. He was, indeed, small—mostly because he was a quadruple amputee—his torso wiggled on a big skateboard.

"And that's Deena," the homeless man pointed to a third individual. To Danny's eyes, she was oddly *okay*-looking. Dirty? Yes. Stinking like diarrhea soup in a blender? Yes. About seven feet five inches tall? Yes. But she did have a kinda pretty face, even though it sported just a single tooth.

"I'm Da-Danny," Danny quavered, shivering. "Would it be alright if I warm up here for a little?"

Lazlo headbutted the air about seven times, which was his version of a nod. "Sure thing! Come close!"

Danny stepped closer, his sludgy arms akimbo at crooked angles, so his hands could continue busying himself with his pubes. Drawing near, he noticed the insides of the metal can glowing, emitting a foul odor, like a toad's puke, and the harsh scent that could only come from burnt... *hair?*

"What's in there?" whispered Danny, feeling the otherworldliness of the place he was in, akin to the otherworldliness of the UFO—such an utter remoteness, feeling adrift like a lone mote in a vacuum.

"Why don't ya bring yer head in closer? Take a good whiff!" said Lazlo.

So, Danny did. And as he did so, he noticed what looked to be an orb—chalk-white, with black holes in it, and some skin, and teeth, and-

"Oh my God!" yelped Danny, finally registering that the homeless sewer people were burning a child.

Before he could run, while still pulling at his pubes, Lazlo clunked him over the head with a brick, and all faded to a coarse, grainy black.

***

Consciousness came with a sharp inhalation, which itself came from a punch in the gut. Deena, the giant, subterranean-Amazonian woman, secured Danny's arms behind his back while Jerry the Small had somehow wrapped his very flexible torso around his ankles.

He couldn't move. Lazlo wailed on his stomach again, his fist feeling like a sledgehammer, barreling through the lining of his innards.

"What is that!?" yelped, Lazlo. "What's wrong with yer Jingle Bells!"

Huffing up some bile, Danny let his head fall, noticing that his shorts were around his ankles and were currently being chewed on by little Jerry. His wang caught the cold breeze like a hitcher's thumb, and his pubes bristled, moving along their geometrical, crop circle-like track, growing to become a curled hedge maze, feeling angry, feeling free.

"You're making a huge mistake!" blurted Danny. "My pubic hairs... We can't let them grow!"

Lazlo sneered and sucked his cheeks. "We? Who's *we*. Tell me, what are these fancy little squigglies you got?"

Kneeling, Lazlo brought his face close to Danny's genitalia and sniffed, *hard,* as though he was taking a bong rip through his nostrils.

"Zesty!" he sniped. "Bring him to the meat barrel, Deena. We're eatin' *gooood* tonight!"

Danny struggled, feeling Little Jeffy, or whatever his name was, chewing on his Achilles tendon. His teeth munched into his flesh, somehow feeling both wormy and sharp within.

Trying to whip his body left, and then right, Danny was crestfallen to see that he'd gone in neither direction. Deena had an almost steel-like grip on him.

The warmth of the burning child, nor the stink of its crisping hair, provided no comfort as Danny was dragged, and his fast-growing pubes provided even less solace since he knew, just *knew*, deep down in his loins, what they were capable of.

"LET ME GO!" he shouted. And the sewer bums laughed. Deena began pushing Danny's head toward the putrid, orange flame, until-

"What the fuck!" she howled, suddenly letting go of Danny's arms to clutch her pussy.

Falling over, plopping into a stinking puddle of liquified rat carcasses, Danny rolled to his back and looked up, seeing that long strings of his pubic hair had entered Deena, and they were flowing, crimped length by crimped length, undulating and penetrating, filling her up.

Deena howled! So did Lazlo—although his noise was more of a shriek, and Jerry the Small began flopping, doing his best to wiggle away.

When Deena's eyes started to bulge from her skull, Lazlo moved forward with the brick he'd reacquired, lifting it up high as the burning barrel splashed his body with flickering, magma-like hues.

Danny shut his eyes, expecting to be smashed square through the nose till the brick exited the scruff of his neck, but instead-

Nothing came, save for some rustling, struggling sounds, and choked gurgles. The pubes flowing from his crotch tickled, he could feel that they were still *going*, and *growing*, so he opened his eyes, only to see Deena's face breaking open like a gory puzzle, each piece becoming a travesty of the human form.

With some popping crunches, bloody froth and chips of skull oozed forth from her mangled face, twitching atop the sopping, still-writhing pubes.

Lazlo didn't fare any better, the strands of short but now long hairs unfurled themselves up his asshole while he jittered on his elbows and knees.

Then, much like Deena, the top of his skull cracked wide to upchuck a spew of hairy brains which splatted on the damp concrete.

Kind of escaping, Jerry the Small had wiggled a distance, kerplunking into the churning, green-black river that swelled through the sewer, bobbing and choking, unable to paddle to keep his head above the liquid sick.

Danny watched the gurgling torso vanish, turd-like, down the tube. He trembled his way to his feet, then swallowed a ball of stress, and looked down.

"Oh... NO!"

His netherhair had extended from his crotch in one long, bumpy wave of horridness.

"Fuck! FUCK!"

Danny hobbled to his left, hoisting the thick, wool-like genital blanket over the burning barrel, singeing his pubes off near his cock, severing them from his body so that they flapped around like innumerable, skinny eels, struggling in the dead homeless, before laying still.

Breathing a sigh of relief, Danny let his face form a tired smile... then his penis caught fire.

***

The flames had moved up his pee hole like an intense, and very sudden, strain of gonorrhea. They charred his cock tip and nut sack so badly that he yowled.

He smacked his beaten genitals with open palms, going *eeee-eeee-eeee*, till the embers subsided, being snuffed in their ports.

The idea of throwing in the towel, the curly, pubic one, reverbed in the pit of his brain. Pain was inevitable, he knew, and there were only two ways to stop this thing.

Keep plucking... or commit suicide. Thinking of the aliens, with their big, wormy faces, he shivered and chose the former.

***

Need to get to higher ground. I told them not to mess with me! I've been telling everybody!

Danny climbed the metal ladder rungs, set into the concrete of the sewer, going for a manhole cover with oval-shaped holes that glittered with an occasional glow. He ascended slowly, using only one hand, while the other one made sure to pinch out any new sprouts from his crispy manscape.

Keep going. Keep going, damn you!

Reaching the top, he used the back of his neck and his shoulder, muscling the heavy cover up and sliding it to the side, hearing it grate against the sidewalk above.

"Free..."

The air gusted like a cold breath that swallowed his filthy body as he emerged. He started trundling forth, down the thoroughfare, keeping to the shadows between the overarching streetlamps.

Listening, as chopper blades whirred overhead.

***

Ear-splitting, came the squeal of rubber tires on tarmac, cutting through the dank-scented night like a shrill blade. Danny pivoted, spotting the white van barreling toward him.

"You've got to be shitting me," he mumbled, hobbling forward, multitasking with his ballbag pruning and his attempted escape.

With the van screeching to a stop, after its door *whooshed* open again, scores of psychiatric workers rushed in Danny's direction, their boots slapping the pavement to make a sound like harsh, slapping rain.

He'd only made it a few feet before a jolt of hot-white agony thrashed his lower lumber. Tackled from behind, Danny slammed face-forward into the ground.

He flailed his limbs, looking up to see his capturers in their white button-up shirts, doing their best to neutralize him.

Plunging a needle in his neck as all vision began to fade. And he swore, staring skyward, that he saw the faces of those big-eyed aliens, sneering with their tiny mouths, while the noodling things wriggled under their flesh.

***

Danny awoke in a white-padded room, his arms crisscrossed, swathed tight against his chest within the confines of a straitjacket. He rocked. And felt his short hairs grow.

"Let ME OUT! You don't understand what you're doing! We're all going to die if my pubes get any longer!" he screeched.

No one answered.

His pubes ballooned the crotch of his pants, pushing the elastic out, curlicuing their black mass into free air. Thousands of wiry hairs inched down his pants too, scratching over Danny's knees and down his shins till they wormed out over his feet and zigzagged across the floor.

"HELP! HELP!" Danny shouted.

Then his pubic hair crawled up the walls and up his shirt, ringing around his neck then over his chin and cheekbones and orbitals.

All became a squiggly, scratchy blanket of unfettered, growing pubes. Danny screamed again, but his cries were snuffed out by his thickening shroud of genital hair.

***

The door creaked open, within its threshold stood a white-frocked psychiatrist, whose name was Dr. Leeman, and a few nurses, also dressed in white.

They all did what Danny could no longer do—shrieking like stuck chinchillas, noticing the overwhelming black puff of pulsating curlies that'd once been a teenager.

Pube-Danny shook, just a supersized, swollen something-or-other that some gargantua might pull out of a shower drain. From the black-curled sphere enveloping his body, lengths continued to grow and fill the room, crawling all about the floor, the walls, and over the ceiling, filling the space with their steady pulse.

Dr. Leeman and the others turned to run, but the pubes flooded through the door, washing over them, wrapping them up, and leaving them ensnared, then continued down the hall.

And soon, the whole mental hospital had become a mass of squirming, *growing*, pubes.

***

City by city, rural landscape by rural landscape, extending across state lines, crossing the borders of countries, the pubic hair continued to grow at an ever-quickening pace.

It coursed over the ocean floor, then reached to its surface, snagging dolphins and angler fish and jellies and the like, bloating to the sky as it swallowed everything in its perennial rustle.

***

Danny jiggled in the white-padded room, unable to move, his pubes having gotten the best of him, and *the entire world.*

In the moment of this dawning realization, Danny realized he should've committed suicide. Should've swallowed a bullet or a tablet of cyanide. Should've hung his neck with a noose or a cord.

He couldn't do that now. Trapped in his bristling cocoon, he was forced to think, and to ponder, and to wonder where it all went wrong.

It was the U-Fucking-O....

If only he hadn't been hiking through the woods that night, when a spaceship resembling a bushy prick and ballbag swooped down, inhaling him with a piss-colored tractor beam, slurping him into the butthole of the vessel.

As his pubes continued to grow, reaching the stratosphere, thermosphere, then exosphere, puff-a-fying the earth, his memories continued to rise like pertinent issues at a town hall.

He recalled the aliens with the wormy things under their grey flesh. Remembered them pressing their puckering, dime-sized mouths to his scared asshole.

Letting their sentient, inner pubes flow into him, infecting him with a version of puberty that would destroy worlds. Dropping him off, nude and covered in coral-colored, semen-like goop, at the centermost point of a crop circle in the middle of Iowa.

A crop circle whose geometric pattern showed earth hitting puberty, then aging out, till death.

Danny wept at the remembrance, his tears running down the matrix of his netherhairs, like dewdrops on a never-ending spiderweb.

His pubes reached Venus then Mercury, swallowing them up, then Mars and Jupiter, devouring them too, then they squiggled their mass through the blackness within the rest of the solar system—eventually reaching the sun, and catching alight.

Like a tiny barrel, burning at the tip of a galactic spiral arm, Danny's pubes hissed and singed and shrunk back, continuing to grow with flame throughout the known universe, incinerating all there is, all there was, and there ever would be.

The cosmos smoldered, reeking of burnt hair.

DEM GHOULISH BLUES

By: Christine Morgan

Some monsters have all the luck.

I mean, shit, pretty much every monster is better off than us.

Look at vampires, for Christ's sake -- okay, phrasing, but you get the gist. For centuries, those suckers were right down there in the creepy crypts where they belonged. Pale corpses, red eyes, long nails, fangs, cold as death, stinking of the grave, eternally hungry for human blood. Pretty damn monstrous, amirite? With the curse element attached, too, so if one got you, you'd be doomed to the same dreadful fate. They'd behead your corpse, pound an ash stake through your heart, and bury you face down in a churchyard with your mouth stuffed full of garlic and roses.

Then along comes that fucking *Stoker* with his gothic emo tragic romance, and suddenly they're cool, they're sexy, they're suave and elegant and classy and mysterious and dark and seductive. Living in castles. Wearing satin capes. Turning into mist and bats and wolves. Living -- so to speak -- the good life. These days, they're a whole entire trope, with fangirls and movies and Muppets and-and-and *breakfast cereals* ...

It's aggravating, that's what it is. Aggravating and unfair. They're undead leeches, is all they are. Leeches, ticks, mosquitoes. But, *nooooo*, let's cast some brooding pretty boy with dark eyeliner or some voluptuous femme fatale, and suddenly panties are dropping and dicks are rising all around the world.

Speaking of which, how about werewolves? Fearsome beasts, agonizing transformations, murderous uncontrollable rage, slavering-maw slaughterhouses, a thousand times worse than the already-dreaded regular wolves. Only, wait, hang on, let's put a spin on it, make it about primal nature and passion and lust, and freedom, wild freedom from the suffocating restrictions of civilized society! Let's all tear off our clothes, run naked through the woods, howl at the moon, have yiffy furpile orgies! Let's have an entire sub-genre of fiction devoted to shifter-porn, as they call it. Which is nothing but loophole bestiality, if you ask me.

Not that you asked me. Not that anybody asks me. But I see it. I see it all, every sick fetish you people get up to.

Mummies are sexy now, thanks to those movies. Then there's demons, fallen angels, the very Devil himself ... supposedly *the* all-time most-evil *ever* ... well, you don't need me to tell you how *that* goes ... the *Lucifer* show, for instance?

Even the fishmen and swamp creatures get their share of the action! Ever since that Black Lagoon business, with gill-boy groping his big finny fingers all over bombshell bikini babes. Earlier than that, if you count merfolk -- real merfolk, not "a sea-crazed lonely sailor will fuck anything, even a manatee" merfolk. Sirens, right there lounging on islands of piled fleshless skulls, how's that for a giant red flag, but, put tits in the picture and they'll line up around the block. Or

Deep Ones! *Deep Ones*, and yeah maybe they have to pay for it with their weird eldritch gold, but still! And don't even get me started on all the squidgy tentacle stuff.

Seriously, it's unbelievable.

You're supposed to be *afraid* of monsters! Not hot for them!

Look at Medusa! No, wait, another bad choice of words there. Except, that was supposed to be the *point*, you know? She was cursed by the gods to be so incredibly *ugly*, so downright *hideous*, that the mere *sight* of her *face* would turn someone to stone. Yet, what have you got now? What have you got? Sultry supermodels with snakey hair, and the turn-to-stone part is all in the eyes. That sunglasses commercial with her slinking along? I could just puke!

All right, all right; technically, I couldn't just puke; it's physically impossible for me to puke. But you know what I mean.

All those Greek 'monsters' were getting laid left, right, and center, going by the stuff you see today. Minotaurs, centaurs, sphinxes, harpies, fauns ... wouldn't surprise me one bit if there's erotica out there where Scylla gives simultaneous blowies to half of Odysseus' crew instead of biting their heads off! And you want loophole bestiality? Leda and the swan, there's classical goddamn *art* of it, paintings, sculptures, this chick getting banged by a big ol' bird, but it's okay because it's Zeus? Puh-lease.

Strayed from monsters to myths a bit, but it's all the same thing. You find it in fantasy, too, and sci-fi. Orcs. Aliens. Dragons! A kid's movie -- a *kid's movie*! -- had a subplot about a donkey fucking a dragon, joking about it, wink-wink-say-no-more!

While we're on the subject of donkeys, how about literature? How about *Shakespeare*? There's Oberon, all, "ha ha made you fuck a donkey," and Titania laughs it off "oh you, you're so cute, let's make up." They teach that one in *schools*!

Sorry, got sidetracked for a second. Thing is, like I was saying, *monsters*! Monsters, and how you're supposed to be *afraid* of them!

Not hot for them, but also, not think they're *cool*!

That's equally aggravating in its own way!

Take zombies, for example. *Zombies*! Shambling cadavers chowing down on the living -- let's not even get *into* the fast-vs.-slow debate -- and turning their victims into more zombies, until it's a full-scale zombie apocalypse. And you romanticize even that! Sure, more in a scary way than a sexy one, mostly, but it's become mainstream, its own industry. People prep for it, look forward to it, can't *wait* for their chance to shoot 'em in the head. Bunch of macho tough-guy survivalist power fantasies run amok.

You nutballs made *zombies* trendy and cool. Zombies. Freakin' zombies. While *we* ...

Maybe I'm a little bitter here, but can you blame me?

All those monsters made famous and popular. Idolized. Imitated, With groupies and wannabes and the works.

Hell, even some of your *human* 'monsters' have that! Serial killers and mass murderers and genocidal maniacs, getting marriage proposals while sitting on Death Row? Unreal. Un-fucking-*real.* Your actual *cannibals* are more famous, or infamous. How many stories are there about inbred hillbillies or remote tribes? How many internet meet-and-eat match sites for sick hookups? Some of you will pony up insane amounts of money for an empty Tupperware container from Dahmer's freezer. There's an actual-goddamn-Broadway-*musical* with a catchy number about baking people into meat pies and it's been running for *decades*!

Fictional supernatural slashers like Freddy and Jason? Naked pin-up fanart, themed dildos, slutty Halloween costumes ... well, there's slutty Halloween costumes for almost everything now; slutty M&Ms, slutty laundry detergent, whatever. Anyway!

It's unreal. What is *wrong* with you?

Ghosts, okay ... for the most part anyway, ghosts at least remain generally scary. Barring certain tragic love stories with pottery wheels and such shit. Ghost-hunting is bigger than ever. Asian ghost girls, creepy dolls? Legit terrifying. Which, fine, great, good for them. As it should be. But, why should they get so much attention while other, equally-deserving monsters go without?

Side note -- by the way, it's just plain stupid to think cemeteries are haunted. Ghosts don't hang around there. It's where they died, or where they lived and left their unfinished business; that's what binds them. Take it from me; I've spent a lot of time in cemeteries, and hardly ever run into a ghost at any of them.

You know who else has plenty of cred? Cryptids. Cryptid-cred. Whether it's Bigfoot -- oh and there's porn, there's *soooo* much Bigfoot porn! -- or Nessie, or Mothman, or the Jersey Devil, or even the goddamn goat-sucking *Chupacabra*, they've got the cred. They've got the media mystique. Bat-Boy, from the *Weekly World News,* is practically a celebrity in his own right!

We're monsters too, is what I'm trying to say here. What about *us*? Where's *our* movie franchises, graphic novels, and Netflix series?

And we're *real* monsters! As opposed to, say, natural creatures like dinosaurs or spiders or sharks ... let alone mad-science crap like *Octodactylantula vs. Waspasaurus.*

We've been here as long as any of the others, and longer than some! We've been here as long as *you* people have! All the way back to your mud huts and cave-dwelling days! Right there with you, through thick and through thin, through droughts and plagues and Ice Ages and Industrial Revolutions.

Eons! Epochs!

And this is the thanks we get.

Ignominy at best.

Overlooked, ignored, forgotten.

Not sexy.

Not even feared, really.

Not even feared. Loathed, sure. Regarded with disgust and revulsion, okay.

Like maggots. Like worms. Nobody's afraid of maggots or worms. Just grossed out by them.

Do you have any idea how that makes us feel?

No. No, of course you don't. And you wouldn't care if you did.

In fact, I wonder sometimes if we even *count* as monsters anymore.

Did we ever?

After all, it's not like we made a practice of hunting you, killing you. It's not like we could bite you and turn you into one of us, or possess you, or corrupt your soul.

We just eat your dead.

And not even your fresh dead. We weren't out there on the battlefields alongside the wolves and the ravens, didn't circle with the vultures, or lurk with the hyenas. We waited. We had the common-fucking-decency to wait, to let you mourn and grieve and bury them. Only later, when all was said and done, would we -- quietly, mind you; discreetly! -- dig them up.

Yes, okay, it's because we need them rotted, but that's beside the point.

We don't bother the living. If anything, aren't we doing a public service? Disposing of corpses so they wouldn't fester and pollute and spread sickness and disease?

It would be so much easier on us all if you'd simply ... go with it.

But, noooo.

You have to make such a big goddamn *deal* out of it.

As if eating the rotten, decaying flesh of your friends, loved ones, and neighbors is somehow *bad*.

They're not using it anymore! Why let it go to waste? Take up space? Pose a health risk?

But, noooo.

All your talk about spirits, the afterlife, heaven, or whatnot ... all your talk about ashes to ashes and dust to dust and leaving the bodily shell behind ... yet it always sure does upset you to find a grave unearthed. Desecrated, you say. Defiled, you say.

And the lengths you go to! Good God! The time, effort, and resources you put into making *our* lives more difficult! For what? For a lump of cold meat you have no further need of?

They're *dead*!

The important part, the one your priests bang on about, has moved *on*! To this eternal reward or that eternal punishment or some other bullshit.

Is it sentimentality? Some screwed-up idea of respect? Or is it sheer, selfish, petulant spite? Just have to ruin it for everyone else, is that it?

First, it was simple wrappings. Fine, fair enough. Bundle them into a hide or a shroud, so you don't have to see their slack faces and blank, staring eyes. No problem. We could handle that. Like an extra layer of skin to get through, that was all.

Then you went and started burying them. Again, fine, fair enough. We can dig. These claws of ours, they're made more for digging than fighting anyway. Thick. Wide. Strong. We can burrow through hard-packed earth if we need to; the loose fill you'd cover the grave holes with was no problem. In a way, really, your burying them that way was even beneficial since it did help deter other scavengers. For a while there, it almost seemed as if you were being considerate.

Until you started with the cairns. Piles of stones we had to painstakingly shift aside before digging. Like maybe you weren't being so considerate after all. Like maybe you didn't want us to eat your dead after all. Which, as I've mentioned, is just wasteful, spiteful ... and, honestly, kinda rude.

I mean, we need to eat, too. It's hardly our fault. We didn't *ask* to be this way. We didn't set out to require a diet of rotted human flesh. We're evolutionary specialists. Like koalas. They can only eat eucalyptus, but do you see the world giving them a hard time about it? Do you go around burying eucalyptus leaves under piles of rocks so the koalas have to do extra work for their dinner?

If you think about it, you people have gone to some pretty insane, extreme lengths to try and keep us away from our food source. And you kept upping the ante! From cairns to burial mounds to tombs to fucking marble mausoleums or hundred-foot-high pyramids! When cheap pine-plank caskets only slowed us down some, you escalated to polished and varnished hardwoods ... then lead-lined ... then those Victorian grave cages you *claimed* were meant to prevent grave robbers from selling Aunt Ermengarde to a medical college ... concrete slabs ...

For real, what next? Stainless steel? Titanium? Come *on* already! Do you see these teeth? Yes, we can gnaw through solid mahogany, but it's no goddamn picnic. Takes a while, too. You ever try tearing open stubborn food packaging when you're starving? You know how infuriating it is!

Oh, but wait, said humanity, but wait, there's more. More ways we can fuck the ghouls over! What if we burned the dead? Hey, yeah!

Funeral pyres! Incinerators! Cremation! Talk about insult to injury. Perfectly good corpse, ready to ripen and rot into a tasty meal, enough to feed one of us for a week or more, but you'd rather *set it on fire* and *char it to cinders,* so it's no use to anyone? Assholes.

Burial at sea? Oh, yes, very nice. Chuck 'em into the ocean. Do we look like we can swim? You'd rather be torn to shreds by sharks, their bones and ragged scraps settling to the ocean floor to be picked at by eels and crabs because somehow you think that's preferable? What did we ever do to you to make you treat us like this?

Oh! And while I'm on the subject ... while I am on the subject ... embalming. Embalming. Em-fucking-*balming.* What. The. Hell. Whose goddamn bright idea was it to drain out a corpse's blood and pipe in a few gallons of nasty chemical shit? Listen, maybe *you* like your food loaded with preservatives -- those of you who aren't into the whole healthy organic free-range whatever -- but who said you could go and force your lifestyle choices on *us*, huh? As if already being chock-full of caffeine and booze and nicotine and high-fructose corn syrup, not to mention drugs and other medicinal or 'recreational' substances aren't enough? That shit permeates your tissues, you know. It lingers.

Which *also* reminds me! Tattoos. Used to be, they'd only show up on sailors and bikers and tribal types, but now damn near everybody's got them! Kids! Grandmas! For some of us, you know, the skin's our favorite part, but not when it's full of artificial colors and flavors!

Can't you just live and die and rot normally? Is that so much to ask? Do you have to deny us these most basic necessities and simple pleasures?

Though to be fair, lately there has been more of a movement toward 'green' burials, with the biodegradable shrouds and fungus and such, eco-friendly, back to nature, etc. That, yes please, we're all in favor! If you all did that, we wouldn't have anything to complain about. Too bad so far it's mostly the tree-hugger vegan hippie types. The rest of you are still too selfish.

Selfish, yes, I said it. So selfish, in fact, most of you still won't even donate your organs to save some other human's life! Again, not as if you'd be using them anymore, but here comes that miserly possessive streak ... you're all "but it's *my* liver/kidneys/corneas/heart! Those sick kids can fuck off!"

For, I reiterate. your *own kind*! For the sake of fellow living humans, yet you can't be bothered. Selfish. Totally, greedily, horribly selfish. The very idea of even such a good and noble cause is more than you can handle.

Let alone having your inert, decaying flesh go toward, say, feeding a hungry ghoul. Better we should starve? Bunch of Scrooges. Decrease the surplus population, my ass ... we don't have a surplus population ... we're an endangered species, though you also won't see any fundraisers or charitable organizations on our behalf. "For just pennies a day, *you* could make all the difference, join now and get this free t-shirt!" Yeah right.

Then, oh, then, you've also got these cadaver farms, which is just cruel. Rub it in, why don't you? Consent to rot in the name of science, so forensic experts can study the decomposition process under various circumstances ... observing the maggots, blowflies, and worms doing their thing ... tell you, though, if one of *us* turned up? They'd raise holy ol' hell.

So, there we are, stuck outside the barbed wire fences and security cameras they've got all over those places. While dozens of tasty corpses are rotting in shallow graves, or blatantly exposed to the elements ... or locked in the trunk of a car, simmering in their own juices, as the fat liquefies and the meat just slides right off the bone -- whoa, sorry, got carried away there.

But yeah. Those, or countless other crime-scene scenarios. Mere yards away! Their aroma wafting on the wind -- think of how you feel when you pass a pizza place, or a donut shop ... and imagine how it'd feel to know they wouldn't let you in, wouldn't even let you scavenge the dumpsters out back.

Think about it, would you? Just humor me for a minute and think about it. Think about when you sit down for a nice meal. The anticipation. The sensory experience. Sight, scent, flavor, texture, mouthfeel ... I mean, you want umami? Finding one where the rot is just right, just at peak putrefaction? Nothing else like it in the world.

Now, to be sure, each of us has our own diverse preferences, same as you do. Some of us crave the chewy stiffness of rigor, some are into the slick-and-slimy, some enjoy gnawing through to the marrow, some like crunching into the cartilaginous ears or noses, or the brittle little pinkies and toes. It also varies depending on our mood. You can understand that, too, can't you? One day, you might want high-end gourmet fine dining ... another day, only some fast-food greasebomb will do the trick ... yet another day, something light and lean and healthy.

Me, personally? My all-time favorite? Oh, definitely a nice plump buttock or the back of a thick thigh, when the corpse has been face-up so the blood settles into the lower portions. Makes the meat so dark, so rich and moist and spongy. Like a slab of triple-chocolate cake, dense and decadent, not too sweet, with that tang of iron ...

Was that my stomach? Jeez, that was loud. Been a while since I last ate. Probably should change the subject.

Where was I?

Ah, can't remember. Doesn't matter. What it comes down to is, basically, us ghouls, we get the short end of the stick, and it sucks.

None of you think we're cool or scary. Only repulsive, revolting, loathsome, gross. Nobody wants to fuck a ghoul -- which, okay, who could blame you? Who'd want to fuck a big grey naked mole rat? Heard us described once as "turds with feet and teeth," and, unflattering though it is, I can't really say it's far wrong. We don't even like to fuck each other. Part of why we're solitary. Part of why we're endangered.

But we still want to survive! To *exist*! To have some recognition, some basic fucking *respect*, how about it? I'm not saying we need fame and fear and pervy fans -- though we wouldn't turn it down -- but we're sick and tired of being treated like bottom-of-the-barrel monsters not even worth anyone's time. When even the oozing amorphous *blobs* are more popular ...

What's it gonna take, huh? Is it because we *don't* hunt and kill you? Is it because we're *not* contagious, able to turn you with a bite? What do we have to do, here?

Really, when you think about it, you've only got yourselves to blame. If you're not going to romanticize, demonize, or idolize us the way you do the vampires and ghosts and everyone else, you could at least leave us the hell alone. Let us feed in peace, instead of doing every-damn-thing in your power to make it more difficult, for no good reason!

That's all I'm saying. Is it really so much to ask?

We're monsters too, goddamnit. We're monsters too.

Or maybe it's been you people who were the real monsters all along.

The Night of the Living Not Gonna Die but Keep on Living People Who I Couldn't Kill

By Damien Casey & Kyra R. Torres

This one was gonna be great. Y'all have no fucking idea what I had planned. I bought this giant-fuck-you knife. Borderline machete kind of thing. I'm not calling it that though because that makes people think I idolize that Voorhees character. Dude is B-O-R-I-N-G.

I needed a little flair.

A little glitz.

Something that spoke to the soul.

Art.

It's fucking art, K?

It's not the killing that I like, it's the build-up to it!

All the gore and guts and sliced flesh and broken bones and missing teeth and cut in half fingers and opened up rib cages and melting skin with a hair dryer and dropping weights on someone's nuts and puking up shit piss blood cum into a mouth until they suffocate and stabbing people with their own mom's femur and baking baby pies and eyeballs in martinis and smothering with a plastic bag and throwing bricks into traffic and cutting off someone's ear and making them eat it with ranch dressing and frozen pickles stabbed into eyes and toothpicks jammed into tongues and blood blood blood and wrapping myself up with intestines like I'm a mummy trying to impersonate Lady Gaga's meat dress and scooping someone's tongue outta their goddamn mouth with an aluminum pop can that's been ripped in half.

All that shit.

That's my shit.

Then they die and it's just meat.

I tried munching down on it once.

Fucking gross dude!

Spoiled chocolate milk on top of garlic bread levels of gross.

My knife was so fucking big.

Almost phallic.

It was like my ding-a-ling.

This is supposed to be subtext, but who wants any of THAT shit!

WE WANT BLOOD VIOLENCE RIPPED FLESH BATHTUBS FILLED WITH SEVERED TOES AND CHIPPED TEETH.

I snuck up behind her.

I stabbed this giant—totally represents my dong— knife right in her left ass cheek.

She fell forward screaming.

I grabbed the knife and whipped it back and forth across her back like I was making a grid for us to play Battleship on.

Eventually, she stopped screaming out, so I sliced her Achilles' tendons.

Fun fact: when you sever that it sounds like a gun going off.

"Did you shoot me?" she asked.

"Nah, fam, that's your fucking Achilles' tendons!" I told her.

"I didn't feel anything."

"What?"

"I don't feel anything anymore. I'm all numb."

"You should ACTUALLY be dead, bruh."

"Dead I am not, BRUH. How much blood have I lost?"

"A lot."

"What's the fucking deal with this anyway?"

"I don't know. You're a medical miracle."

"No, why are you trying to kill me?"

"I'd rather you didn't die, actually. I just like the goopy ooey gooey gore. The more violent and gore-soaked the better!"

"Oh."

"So, you can like go if you want. I think you're all out of blood."

"Thanks for that. I was actually on my way to donate. I guess THAT plan is ruined."

I watched her walk away.

Her blood was the water at Niagara and her flesh was the barrel filled with a stuntman.

She didn't die.

None of them died.

This was the night of the living not gonna die but keep on living people who I couldn't kill.

This one was going to be good, trust me, it really was. This one offers the perfect setting for the nasty, bloody, raunchy, inappropriate, not-suitable-for-children, not-safe-for-work, XXX.

Watching your dad sneak to the back of the movie store, the beaded 90's curtain swaying as he enters, offering you a glimpse at a VHS with the words, Wet, Horny Sluts.

Two girls with the biggest tits you've ever seen teasing their male audience on the cover.

Wet, sloppy, painful kisses as I pinned her to the slimy wall of the dark alley behind the local bar. Inside I bought her a drink, and she guzzled it down. Of course, she did. She was that kind of girl. The one who knew she looked good doing it and wanted to get laid.

And I was gonna be the one to do it!

Me and my knife.

Similar in length to the guy on the VHS tape that was hidden in my dad's bedside table.

He WISHES his knife was that big.

I knew she wanted it.

I could practically hear her begging for it between breaths.

"You want this big knife?" I ran it down her cheek, bright red blood a shade darker in the night began leaking from the slit of skin.

"Um, no not really. Also, can you maybe not do that? I really don't want it to scar."

"I'm trying to kill you and you're worried about a scar?"

But I knew she wouldn't die.

Still, I made the effort by piercing the long, hard steel into her gut. The taut, smooth skin spread open for me as we both moaned together.

Did she actually like this?

"You're not supposed to enjoy this!"

I ripped through her the same way you rip open a bag of your favorite chips when you want a little snacky snack in the middle of the afternoon, and her sticky intestines begin to spill out all over the filthy, cobblestone street.

"Gross! That's what they look like?" She gathered them in her hands and held them close as if they were a newborn baby.

"They smell funny."

I think I'm going to puke just remembering this.

"Can you maybe not smell them? It's really grossing me out."

She looked up at me with eyes full of rage and I knew I fucked up.

"You're grossed out? You took me back here to slice me up, gut me like a fucking pig, probably take my liver home and eat it while you watch the newest episode of Saturday Night Live, but YOU'RE grossed out?! Unreal."

I thought killing people was going to be fun and I was going to get to see all kinds of gruesome shit, but it's sort of starting to become annoying.

"Not to mention I thought you were gonna fuck me! Why don't you just stab me in the heart and kill me like a real man?"

So, I did.

The blade went in like cheese and we both just stared at each other.

She still didn't die.

"I'm gonna send for an Uber and see if they can take me to the hospital to get these put back or something. Hopefully, they won't mind if I get blood all over their car."

She gripped the knife and pulled it out slowly before handing it back over to me.

"Hey, don't ever hit me up on Tinder ever again. This was the worst one-night stand of my life."

I think she might be a real psychopath.

"Feel like a real fucking moron, don't cha?"

This bitch again. The first one.

"Didn't I already kill you? Fuck off please."

"So polite for a guy who forgot two things: first, I can't die; second: you fucked up my whole day! I can't go donate blood now. I'm as dried up as that poor woman's pussy was when you started that dirty talk!"

"It wasn't dirty talk. It was the truth."

"Et wa'ant dartay tok!"

"Leave Me alone!!!!!"

But she didn't.

She followed me.

I turned around and stabbed the knife up through the bottom of her jaw, all the way up onto her skull.

She jumped no more than if I had popped out of a darkened corner and said "BOO!"

She ripped the knife from her jaw and threw it down.

"You... ASSHOLE!" She shrieked.

"Is there a problem?"

Oh great.

An old man.

Old dapper Dan the old wise man on the fucking case.

"Go have a heart attack, you stupid old fuck!"

"Funny you mention that..."

"Oh. My. God. He had a heart attack!" yelled the First Lady.

That's her name.

I'm the president of violence and she is my bride.

"I didn't die though..." old fart said.

I shoved him to the ground and sliced his face off like pizza toppings.

He screamed and ran so far away he must be in another country.

I picked up the face.

I cut two chunks of First Lady's hair.

I tied the face over my face like a mask.

"Whoa!" yelled First Lady. "Geezer face! Far fucking out!"

A pickup truck pulled up behind us.

Four men climbed out.

"It's like a clown car," said First Lady.

"You try to kill my sister, bub?" asked one of four dudes holding weapons. His is a tire iron. Very cliche.

"Sure. Why not?" I said as I started swinging my knife.

I bounced around from weapon to weapon. My face is the pinball, and their weapons are the paddles.

My mask flew off at one point.

I fell to the ground, blood pouring from my wounds.

I looked over and saw a woman in a nightgown holding an iron.

"Hey, lady," I said, "gonna iron my shirt?"

She swung the thing by its power cord and walloped me over the head.

I stood up and grabbed my mask.

When I put it on the atmosphere changed completely.

I had become a badass.

I mean, I was before then too, but totally one after.

I stabbed the old woman in her fucking eye. When she fell, I took the iron and did the same trick she did. Thanks for the lesson, you crazy old dickhead.

It hit two of the dudes and their faces exploded in blood, bone, and teeth.

I wrapped the cord around one's neck and squeezed it until the bones broke.

I picked up my knife and sliced the brother man's head clean off.

I picked it up and held it to my face.

"Now what the fuck am I going to do?" he asked. "I have work tomorrow. I can't go like this. I got no arms or legs! Or body!"

It was hella annoying.

"You're such a fucking idiot," said First Lady.

"This is so boring," I said.

"I figure it's like sex, right? You're doing all the cool shit but there's no cum shot. No orgasm. And you're just sort of doing it to do it. No point to it. It's just pointless boring violence."

I sigh because I know she's right.

I need something more.

***

I've got it. That final scene where the camera pans out and the POV gets ready for that big money shot. The one you're breathing really heavy for, sweat beading across the forehead of a grown man still living in his uncle's house.

Here it comes.

Get ready!

It's a mess.

First Lady stood over me, the light shining through the window making her look like an angel.

An angel of death.

Eh, kind of.

"Harder."

Her arm bobbed up and down. Each stroke got me closer to the feeling I had been chasing when I started this day.

"I said harder!"

The mask slid over, and the flesh covered one of my eyes.

I felt like a pirate for a second which only made me feel even cooler.

"Almost there!"

A giant SNAP filled the room, and the pain was unbearable but offered the climax I'd been looking for.

She held up my leg and the exposed bone was also white against the blood dripping onto my leaking cock.

It brought a tear to my one eye.

"Is that better?"

"Sort of. I need more."

She looked over to the pile of limbs. Some mine, some belonging to the others.

All stacked neatly into a mountain of gore and flesh and blood.

It was so edgy.

Some might even say, "spooky."

"Are you sure you want me to take more? Don't you have to go to work tomorrow or something?"

"Yeah, I guess."

"Do you need arms to drive or anything?"

"Well, maybe just one."

"Can we remove your head?"

"I'll definitely have to call out, but that can be arranged."

She grabbed the knife–my knife–and gripped it in her perfect, blood-stained hand.

I could feel myself getting ready for round two at the sight of the entire thing.

"Hey," I said, "do you think it's the massive pile of body parts, the gore, and the hot chick sawing on me, or is it the love I found along the way?"

She shoved a massive firecracker in my mouth and set it off.

Fecesnura
The Demon Lord of Shit

By: Tony Evans

Franklin sat in the corner booth of the Main Street Diner and stared off into the distance. He wasn't just staring, though. Not at nothing. Not the way people do when their mind is just wandering. There was one thing across the room holding his attention; it was the one thing in the entire world that could always keep his focus and make him forget about all the shitty things the day may have thrown his way, which, in his case was quite a lot...and quite often.

This *thing*, of course...the one that held his focus so intently...was, of course, a girl. What else would a puberty-ridden teenage boy occupy his mind with? Especially one as horny as poor ol' Franklin Douglas.

Her name was Rose, and she didn't have to be doing anything special to make him all giddy and fluttery inside. In fact, just the mere sight of her serving an elderly couple across the room carried him off to another world; a world that he often struggled to distinguish from reality. When it came to Rose some would say that Franklin was a bit of a daydreamer. She was so goddamn attractive, though. Jesus fucking Christ! She was small and petite, tight in *all* the right places, and she had the sweetest little smile that God, if ever there was one, could've ever thought to grace humanity with. Even the way her silky blond curls reflected the sun as it shined through the window made her look like an angel to him.

Goddamn, she was cute. *Perfect* even, and that's pretty much all there was to say about her in Franklin's eyes.

Someday, Rose, he thought to himself, smiling the smile of most gooning teenage perverts. *Someday we'll be together. Someday I'll run my hands all over that soft, milky-white skin of yours as I bury my face between those sweet little ass chee—*

Before the thought could even be finalized, Rose looked up at him, her eyes squinted, the faint hint of a grin stretching across her ruby lips. She stared for a moment, almost as if she'd heard his thoughts as if they'd somehow made some sort of cosmic connection, though unintentional on Franklin's behalf, and she could suddenly read his mind.

Holy fuck! Franklin thought, his eyes widening as Rose turned and started in his direction. His heart rate began to increase as he racked his brain to come up with a reason...a non-sexual and significantly less perverted one...for why he'd been drooling over her. If, in fact, she *had* read his mind, there was no covering that up. It's hard to come up with excuses and justifiable reasons as to why one would want to bury their face between someone else's ass cheeks. *Fuck, fuck, fuck!* he thought as she got closer. *Think, Franklin. Think of something to say. Why were you looking at her? What were you doing? Nothing stupid either. FUCK!*

It was one of those instances where the whole thing happened in the course of a couple of seconds, but it seemed to drag out over hours in his head. The fear of confrontation, the nervousness he got from it all building up in his mind. But it was inevitable. She was coming straight for him, and her eyes were directly trained on his.

"Hey there, Franklin," she said, the sound of her voice almost sweet enough to melt him into a puddle. "You weren't lookin' my way, were you?" She pouted her bottom lip out, her jade-green eyes nearly hypnotizing Franklin.

"Wha…uh…I-I mea—"

"Shh," she said, placing her index finger against his lips to hush him. "Those were some pretty dirty things goin' on in that brain of yours, hmm big boy?" She winked and blew a kiss. "I'd be lyin' if I said it didn't turn me on a little. Nothin' in the world like havin' your asshole eaten. Ain't that right, Frankie?"

His heart nearly beating a tattoo on his chest, Franklin froze as he stared in disbelief at what was happening. Rose was there, right in front of him, saying things he'd only dreamt of. Her finger was even *touching* his lips!

"Mmm," she moaned. "Just trust me when I tell you that I *love* the feeling of a tongue flicking across my asshole."

His eyes twitching from side to side, Franklin looked around, confused as fuck. He ran through various scenarios in his mind trying to make sense of it all. This couldn't be real. There was no fucking way it was. Maybe she was mistaking him for someone else. Someone that maybe looked similar. But if that were the case, why did she say his name? The odds of someone else with the same name and having similar features in the same town they lived in were very low, but it *had* to be a mix-up. *Had* to be. He knew he wasn't Rose's type. She was into the muscular type. The athletes. The *jocks*, as the general population tends to call them. Not the likes of him. But it wasn't impossible. Stranger things *had* happened.

As Rose stood there looking down at him, he decided that there was only one way to find out for sure. A nervous grin crept across his face, and he nodded hesitantly back at her. "Y...you talkin' to me?"

She raised an eyebrow and chuckled. "Why, who else would I be talkin' to? You're the only Franklin I know. I mean, you *were* lookin' at me, right? Those naughty little thoughts weren't for anyone else's ears, were they?" she asked with a playful frown.

"Well...uh...I mean..."

"I know they were meant for me, silly." She sat down next to him and placed her hand on his thigh, squeezing it forcefully as if she were about to give him some sort of semi-erotic massage. "Oooh, what do we have here? Why, Frankie...is that a summer sausage in your pocket, or are you just happy to see me?" She snickered at her own joke, sliding her hand further up his thigh. "Wow! Nice and juicy, too." She licked her lips again, this time making direct and intentional eye contact. "Just how I like 'em."

A warmth rushed over Franklin that started in his groin and spread quickly into his stomach, eventually radiating throughout his entire body in massive pulses. He'd felt this sensation countless times before, but it was always when he was alone in his room looking at pictures of her. He'd dreamed of something like this happening countless times, but he never thought in a million years that it actually would. Yet here he was sitting in a booth in the Main Street Diner, and Rose was stroking his rock-hard cock through his khakis.

"Mmmmm, I never knew you had such a massive dick, Frankie. *Thick* and *hard*," she said with a sultry whisper. Scooting closer, she slid her tongue around his ear lobe, caressing it gently as she nibbled.

Franklin grunted and began thrusting his hips back and forth as his cock throbbed with pleasure. Rose looked at him and he could tell that she was enjoying it almost as much as he was. Everything else around them seemed to disappear. The other servers, all the guests, and patrons of the restaurant. Everything and everyone except Rose and him. All he could hear now was a static-like roar that seemed to get louder with each passing second, engulfing every other sound but Rose's sweet voice. The feeling was too much for Franklin to take. Her hand felt so good on his cock as she stroked up and down its length through his pants. The sweet scent of vanilla filled his nostrils as she continued leaning into him, whispering unimaginable thoughts into his ear.

"I-uh…you should probably s-stop, Rose. I-I me…uh…oh no!" He was thrusting his hips uncontrollably against her hand now and his face flushed a deep fever red. He grunted again, trying to fight it, but her voice, her scent, her gentle yet aggressive touch was enough to send him over the edge. "Uh...I-I'm...I'm cumming, Rose!" he yelled out as he felt his cock explode pumping pulse after pulse of hot, thick, creamy jizz into his pants. "Aaaaaahhhhhhh!"

His body fully relaxed as a result of what had just been the best and most intense orgasm of his young life, Franklin sat there in the booth with his eyes closed. After a few seconds, a realization suddenly began to dawn on him. Little by little, his ears began to pick up sounds again. Not just him and Rose, but all the normal sounds of a diner. Music playing on the jukebox, the bell ringing as the door opened and closed. It all came creeping back. But there was one sound that seemed to cut through all the rest. One specific sound that stood out to Franklin above all others. A sound that sent a sudden shock directly into his system.

The sound of laughter. Loud, deafening, ear-piercing laughter that echoed throughout the entire room.

A sudden surge of adrenaline pumped through Franklin's body as he began to realize what had just happened. He opened his eyes and saw Rose standing before him holding a pitcher of soda. The look on her face was not a good one. It was one that signaled pure and absolute disgust.

"Jesus Christ!" she yelled to him. "I asked if you needed a refill. Not if you wanted to bone! Holy shit, Franklin. Keep it in your pants, you pathetic little pervert!"

"Wha-huh?" Franklin looked around to see a fully occupied dining room. His legs started to quiver as his fight-or-flight response kicked in. "Oh no. This...this isn't real. It *can't* be!"

The entire room roared with laughter.

"Shut up," he yelled back at them, turning his attention to Rose. "Please, Rose. I...I'm really sorry. I...it's not what you think. I mean, I'm not a pervert, I promise." In an attempt to explain himself and save what little face he could, not that there was much he could save now, he stood from the booth and reached out his hand as if begging her. "Rose, please. I—"

The look on her face, as he extended his hand, was a mix of utter horror and hilarity, and it didn't take long for everyone else in the restaurant to follow suit, pointing at him and laughing.

"What?" he shouted. "Why are you all pointing at me?" He stood there surveying the room in confusion, finally realizing where everyone was pointing. All of their fingers were pointing down. Pointing at his lower half. "Holy shit...please tell me it isn't happening." He looked down, and what he saw was nearly enough to stop his heart. The crotch of his khakis had stained a dark tan color from something wet. It looked as if he'd pissed himself. But he knew it wasn't piss. He knew from the daydream, from the feel of a warm and slimy substance slipping down his leg, the tenderness of his still semi-bulging cock.

His heart accelerated and his breathing grew shallow and fast.

"Minute man!" one boy yelled out. "Look at Frankie the minute man!"

"Look everybody, it's good ol' Fappin' Franklin," another said, causing the crowd to laugh even louder.

Franklin didn't so much care about the rest of them. He was used to being laughed at and picked on. The worst part of the whole thing, the part that really *hurt* him, was that Rose was laughing, too, and she was laughing harder than everyone else. In this moment in time, it was like she was using him for nothing more than her own personal comic relief.

His beloved Rose.

"Geez, what a little perv!" she said. "I know I'm hot, but goddamn! Creaming your pants just because I asked if you wanted a refill? You really need to get laid, loser!"

"No, Rose. D...don't do this. Please. Not like this," he pleaded.

"Like you could ever have a piece of this!" she yelled back, reaching around to slap her own ass.

He felt his lower lip quiver and his hands started to shake as a single tear rolled down his cheek. All around him, they were laughing. An endless roast he'd never intended to be a part of or even invited to. He turned and ran toward the door, determined to get out of the diner and back to the safety of his own room as fast as possible. "Out of my way!" he cried, flailing his arms wildly. "Just leave me alo—"

The feeling hit him like a brick; a quick, sharp, forceful strike to his stomach. Gasping for breath, he looked to his side and saw Jimmy McCloud, Rose's current *thing*, sitting in a booth next to him.

"Aww. That hurt little buddy?"

"L-leave me—" He tried to speak, but he was nauseous now, his stomach rolling like a series of waves in a tsunami. "I'm gon-I'm gonna...throw—" In a violent spasm, his lunch spewed from the pit of his stomach, exiting his mouth as if being shot out of a cannon, landing all over Jimmy. Heave after heave, bits of cheese and pepperoni mixed with milk and bile made its way from Franklin's gut onto Jimmy's lap.

In a collective sigh, the entire restaurant went silent.

"Why, you little son-of-a bitch!" Jimmy yelled. He stood up, sending a cascade of chunky puke crashing to the floor. "I'll fuckin' kill you!" He punched Franklin in the face this time, unfortunately getting a mixture of blood and vomit on his hand. "That'll teach you to hurl on me you little motherfucker. Fucking disgusting little shit!"

Franklin spun around and hit the ground hard, causing the mess of vomit he'd just made on the floor to splash up. He groaned and tried to push himself to his feet, but his hands kept slipping on the lumpy concoction.

"Stay down there and lick it up off the floor!"

His face scrunched in both pain and disgust, Franklin let out a cry causing everyone to laugh and taunt him even more.

"I said, *lick* it," Jimmy commanded, forcing Franklin's head against the floor with his boot. "That's a good boy."

In his cries, the thick yellow and white mess lurched its way back into his mouth as he gasped for air. He gagged and blew it out as best he could, but it was no use.

"And let this be a lesson to ya. Leave Rose alone from now on. She's my piece and she don't want nothin' to do with you, ya fuckin' little loser pervert." He snorted and hocked, swishing a huge ball of mucous around in his mouth. He took Franklin's hair in his fist and pulled his head back so that he could look him in the eyes. Then, with all the force he could muster, he let the loogie fly.

A deafening splat echoed in the room as a giant, bright green ball of mucousy snot slapped against Franklin's cheek.

"Next time, I'll be force feedin' ya my *shit*. And if ya think I'm jokin', just try me."

"Leave me alone!" he screamed, finally able to free himself and get to his feet. "You'll be sorry, Jimmy, you and Rose both! You'll see. You'll be sorry you ever laughed at me!" Slipping and sliding in the nasty mess, Franklin ran out the door leaving a trail of vomit-stained footprints behind.

   ***

Franklin scowled as he paced back and forth in his room. "Eat your shit, huh? We'll see about that, *Jimmy*. We'll just see how that works out for you. And Rose." He opened a picture of her on his phone, one he'd taken nearly a year ago without her knowing. "How *could* you? Making a goddamn fool of me in front of *everyone* like that. I fucking loved you!" His eyes squinted, he shook his head in disgust, in heartbreak. "You've done it now, though. Nobody humiliates me like that and gets away with it. Your time will come, too. We could've been so happy together." Out of nowhere, there was movement in his pants, and a feeling of excitement coursed in his loins. A sinister grin stretched across his face as his dick continued to shift position, stiffening effortlessly. "What's that," he said, still staring at the picture of Rose. "You thought I was mad at you? Oh, Rose," he chuckled. "Sure I may hate you now, but that doesn't change the fact that you're hotter than fuck. And, well, I'll still rub one out to you. More than one, actually."

He placed his hand on the crotch of his pants and started rubbing, but before he was able to really get into it, a crusty feeling on the fabric reminded him of the recent tragedy. "Goddamnit," he said, realizing what it was. He looked down to find the area was covered in dried semen from earlier. It had formed a flaky white patch when it dried. "Fucking assholes. I've gotta get them back somehow. Eat his shit. Yeah, right. Like he could actually make me do that. What a fucking prick. What I *should* do is—"

He paused mid-statement, a thought coming to him. It wasn't just any thought, though...it was genius. The *perfect* thought. Perfect for this situation, and even more than perfect for the likes of Jimmy fucking McCloud. Franklin grinned, the edges of his mouth curling up like those of a cartoon villain. "That's it," he said, an almost sinful whisper in his voice. "Why didn't I think of it sooner? It's the perfect revenge. Disgusting, vile, horrifyingly beautiful...in its own way, of course, and just goddamn perfect."

He hurried over to his laptop and opened the browser. He stared down at the screen, a hauntingly devilish look in his eyes as his fingers typing away at what seemed like superspeed. "Eat *your* shit, huh, Jimmy? Well, how about I do you one better?" He started laughing maniacally, a sound that ventured into the realm of what most would call psychopathy. It was so loud, so horrifyingly crazy sounding that any normal person passing by would almost certainly think he was a few marbles short of a full set. "How about I make *you* eat *my* shit! How about that, fuckface?"

Franklin was right. This was a genius plan. Especially as far as revenge was concerned. Or at least he'd convinced himself that it was. Though, revenge can skew one's decision-making abilities significantly. It was still a good plan regardless, but it wasn't without fault. There was one specific problem that came to mind; a rather large one, in fact. Jimmy was a big guy. He was taller, stronger, and more athletic than Franklin in almost every way. So how was he going to make it happen? What was he supposed to do, force feed Jimmy a big ol' turd? There was no way in hell that would fly. No. If he was going to do this, if he was going to make Jimmy McCloud eat his shit, he was going to have to do it the smart way.

He typed in every food item he could think of that looked anything remotely like feces, placing the word *shit* in front of it. He tried shit cookies, shit brownies, and even shit truffles, though he wasn't even sure what the hell a truffle was, but none of the results suited him. Sure, he found several pictures of random items that *looked* like shit, but he already knew they looked like it. He needed recipes. He needed to know how to make these items while mixing his own bodily waste into them. He even tried the phrase *how to make an asshole eat shit*, but that one brought up results that no person should ever see. As it turns out, the internet is full of all sorts of...fetishes...if you will. Fetishes that, even considering all the things he'd imagined doing with Rose, made him gag.

As he scrolled through the various images of chocolate-based items that happened to resemble poop, a thought occurred to him. It came from something he'd seen in a movie a few years ago, something very similar to what he was trying to accomplish now. In the movie, a housekeeper had grown tired of dealing with her employer's assholishness, so she decided to quit, but not before baking a chocolate cake with her own shit in it.

"Yes," Franklin whispered. "That's it! I'm going about this all wrong. I don't have to find a recipe specifically for *shit* food. I just need a recipe for something that *looks* like shit." That option seemed very doable and significantly easier. He could just learn how to make cookies or brownies or something similar, something easy, and load it up with his own stinky ass cream. So long as the item was chocolaty and brown, the color of shit should blend in well and go unnoticed until it was too late.

In the browser, he changed the focus to extra chocolatey foods. "Yes...that'll do just fine," he said, clicking on a recipe for double chocolate fudge brownies. It was a basic recipe, one that even Franklin, a less than stellar baker at best, should be able to follow with relative ease. His grin stretching from ear to ear, he moved the pointer to the print icon and lifted his finger, but just before he clicked the mouse, he noticed something else on the screen. Something that wasn't part of the background. Something that wasn't supposed to be there.

"What...is that?" he leaned closer to the screen to get a better look. His eyes squinted; he concentrated on the image as it slowly came into focus. "What the fuck?" he whispered. He stood there, silent, motionless. A good many seconds passed as he tried to make sense of what he was looking at. Then it moved. Franklin's eyes grew wide as he realized he was staring at a reflection. There was someone, or *something*, standing in the room behind him.

"Why, hello there, Franklin," a wicked voice hissed. "I see you want to get *even*, hmm?" The thing moved again, causing Franklin to jump.

"What the fuck!" he yelled, drawing out the last word as chill bumps crept over the length of his arms. He spun around in the chair to face the intruder; hands balled into fists as he readied to defend himself. "Who the fuck ar—holy shit!" he gasped as he first laid eyes on the intruder. "Wh-wh-what the fu-fu-fuck?" His knuckles turned white as he gripped the chair's armrests tightly, his feet looking for purchase as he scooted back into his desk. He didn't know what it was, but he knew for damn sure that it wasn't a person.

A dirty, skid-mark brown in color, it floated above him, hovering like some sort of dirt-covered fairy. Its skin was lumpy and rough looking, though it seemed to shine in a stomach-churning way as the slightest hint of light caressed its strangely textured yet smooth surface. Its body took no standard shape aside from being awkwardly long and thick. Its legs and arms were short, too, its head the most human-like appendage about it.

"I saw what happened to you today," it hissed. "What a horrible thing that boy did. How embarrassed you must have been...must *still* be."

Franklin sprang from the chair and stumbled toward the door. His head jerked from side to side, his brain unsure of what was happening. "Wh-what the fuck are you? How did you get into my room?"

It smiled at him, revealing rows of little brown nuggets, jagged and worn, in the place of what should have been teeth. "Where do you think you're going? I'm here to help you, Franklin. Don't you wanna get back at them? Come on, it'll be fun. How 'bout it?" It chuckled, forcing a series of loud flatulent spurts from its asshole. With each fart, the stench of sulfur and methane grew stronger, nearly overpowering Franklin.

"What is that *smell*? Goddamn! Make it stop! God, please, make that smell go away!"

The thing looked at Franklin as if offended, but it was more out of annoyance than embarrassment. "Apologies, *boy*. An unfortunate side effect of my rank in the demonic realm. Let me introduce myself. My name, is Fecesnura. I am the demon lord of *feces;* the master of *shit*." Gliding through the air, it came closer to Franklin, offering its hand for him to shake.

"Demon of *feces*? You mean..." Franklin yanked his hand back. Something about the thought of shaking hands with a literal shit demon was a bit unsettling. "But you don't really *look* like a demon. I mean…I thought demons looked, well…different. They're always seducing sexy women in the movies, and they're always rich and powerful. Either that or they look like little red men with pitchfork tails. Pardon me for saying so, but you don't look rich *or* powerful. You look like, well…shit."

Fecesnura hung his head. "Yeah. That's kind of a long story. Suffice it to say, I was a bad little *shit*." He raised his head and stared, eyes burning like coals of fire. "Pun intended. But I digress. Let's get back to business. That's the whole reason I'm here, after all. Business. Do you want to get even with Jimmy, or not?"

"What kind of a question is that? Of course, I wanna get even. That's what I was doing before you showed up. Coming up with a plan to do just that. A *brilliant* plan, if I do say so myself."

"Yes, I know what you were doing. I was watching you. You want him to eat shit, if I'm not mistaken. *Your* shit, to be exact."

"Yeah. That was the plan. Why? Something wrong with it?"

Fecesnura grinned, his fiery eyes narrowing to tiny little slits. "No. Not at all. It's a beautiful plan."

"I thought so," Franklin said, a bit of arrogance in his response.

"I can give you that power if it's what you desire. I can give you the power to make it happen. All you have to do is say *yes*."

Franklin paused, cocked his head to the side. "Wait a minute. If you're a demon, and you're offering me help, aren't you supposed to be trying to steal my soul or something? I mean, you have to want something in return to help me, right? That's how it always is in the movies and stories and such."

"Ha! I'm the lord of *shit*! My freedoms are very minimal. Daddy rarely lets me do anything fun. I have to find *something* to keep me occupied throughout all eternity. This makes for a good distraction. Regarding payment, I wouldn't worry too much. It *is* souls that I feed on, but I'm not particularly interested in yours. Rotten souls for a rotten demon. That's how it works. The soul of the boy who mocked you will be much better than yours. Much more sour and vile. We have *rules*, you know. Even in Hell."

"Rules? But I thought that—"

"Do you want my help or not?"

"Well, I mean—"

"I'll warn you now, though, because it's required. Once you agree, there's no backing out. If you do, it'll be your soul that accompanies me back home, and neither of us wants that. I love souls, but yours is not *rotten* enough. Not *yet*, anyway."

Franklin stood there for a moment thinking about the offer. Dealing with a demon was something he'd never really thought about. Hell, until now, he wasn't even sure he believed in such things. But now, here in front of him, was a real-life honest-to-God demon offering his services. Why not take all the help he could get? Arching his back and jutting out his chest in a sense of dominance, Franklin grinned. "You know what? I don't have anything to lose. The whole school just watched me cream my fucking pants to a goddamn daydream. Rose hates me. She made it perfectly clear that I'm nothing more than a joke to her. Jimmy is probably gonna beat the shit out of me again on Monday, too, and who knows how many more times after that just because he can. Why the hell not? Yes, I could use some help getting him back. Sure!"

Fecesnura's glowing eyes grew wide, an uncomfortably eerie heat radiating from them. "We have a deal then?"

"I said yes, didn't I?"

Holding up his stubby little arm, Fecesnura produced a worn slip of paper, ragged and stained a dull piss-colored yellow. "Follow these instructions exactly as they appear. If you do, then your revenge will be had."

"Don't I have to sign a contract or something? We are making a deal, right?"

"Again, you watch too many movies, boy." He floated higher until he reached the ceiling, smiling down at Franklin. "We have a verbal agreement. That's legal and binding in Hell. As long as you follow through with the instructions, our dealings are done and your soul will remain *yours*. Back out, and, well...things won't be good for you."

"Hmmm. Okay, I guess a verbal contract is good enough. Don't worry, I fucking *hate* Jimmy McCloud. I'd never dream of backing out of this."

"It's been a pleasure, Mr. Franklin. I'll be watching." Fecesnura opened his mouth and a powerful stream of chocolate brown sludge spilled over Franklin, covering him from head to toe.

"Jesus, man! What was that for? You're fucking sick. This smells like *shit*!" He wiped his eyes as best he could, then looked up. Fecesnura was gone. "Great! Leave me another fucking mess to clean up, too."

A demonic laugh echoed in the air. "I told you; I have to find something to keep myself occupied."

***

On the paper was a list of four items, each very specific in nature. Franklin was to collect and mix them together, then consume them before the stroke of midnight. The thought of sweet revenge on Jimmy McCloud, the boy who'd humiliated him in front of everyone, in front of his beloved *Rose*, was too good to pass up. Besides, according to the demon, he had to try now; otherwise, his soul would be doomed to an eternity in *shit* Hell with ol' Fecesnura, and he wasn't sure if he could stomach the smell.

First, it called for something from Franklin's body. This was supposed to bind him to the deed. It was a way to link the revenge to him specifically so that a minimal number of civilian casualties were had. Examples of acceptable items included hair, blood, skin, or other bodily fluid. He decided that a small snip of his own hair would be the easiest to get, so he clipped a chunk from the back of his head and tossed it into a paper cup.

Next, it called for food. Something heavy and dense, preferably high in fiber. This would help *solidify* things and add to the discomfort of the victim. The spicier the food, the worse the victim suffered, and this was something Franklin thoroughly enjoyed the thought of. He went downstairs and opened the refrigerator. He'd remembered having a somewhat spicey dinner a couple of nights ago, and there had to be some leftovers in there somewhere. As he opened each drawer, he scanned the contents, finally finding a log of habanero and jalapeno-infused sausage.

"Not the spiciest, but I guess it'll do."

Third, the list called for a laxative. Franklin went to the medicine cabinet and grabbed what was left of the Milk of Magnesia his dad had used last month when he'd had a bad case of hemorrhoids. His dad had never been one to take many medicines, but he'd complained about the discomfort so much that his mom made him take it. This ingredient, the list said, was to move things along. It had worked for his dad...so it made sense.

As Franklin poured the Milk of Magnesia into the cup with the hair and sausage, he read the final item on the list.

"What the hell?"

He stared at it as if he couldn't read it. It called for something from the body of the victim. "How am I supposed to get that?" He paused, then remembered something in the waste basket beside his bed. "Hmmm." He read over the list again, double-checking acceptable options. "More body fluid, huh?"

He ran back to his room and rummaged around in the trash, pulling a chunk of wadded-up tissue from its depths. "I can't believe I'm doing this." Slowly, he unfolded the cold, wet clump of tissue revealing a sticky green slime. It was the tissue he'd used to wipe the remains of

Jimmy's snot wad from his face. "Well, this *is his* body fluid," he said, tearing off a thumbnail-sized piece and tossing it into the milky-white liquid. "Now, to blend!"

He ran downstairs and grabbed the blender. He added a bit of water to assure there were enough contents to blend and tossed the contents of the cup in. The addition of the sausage made for a thick, lumpy mess, but surprisingly the booger-coated napkin seemed to blend well into the mix. "Great," Franklin said, holding the concoction up in front of him. "This'll feel really good on my tongue. What did I get myself into?"

Holding his nose, he poured the contents into a glass, put it up to his lips, and chugged.

"Now I have to…wait…*what*?"

Franklin read the final task on the list, and he wasn't quite sure that it wouldn't lead to him getting several broken bones. Especially if Jimmy caught him.

"What the fuck," he said, his stomach beginning to growl in opposition. "I gotta get moving."

***

It worked fast.

Within fifteen minutes of downing the nasty sausage and booger juice Franklin found himself squeezing his ass cheeks as he struggled toward Jimmy's house. It was the worst case of the walking shits he'd ever had. With every step the farts seemed to last longer, to get louder and wetter until the familiar feeling of swamp ass consumed him.

"Th-th-this is-uuugggghhhhhh!" Another fart burst from his asshole sending a stream of liquid onto his boxers. "Fuck me!" he screamed. "I'll never ma-make i-eeeewwwwww!" Another fart, another stream of liquid, every toot feeling more and more like a sprinkler shooting out of his colon.

He rounded the corner at Maple and Oak, and there it was, shining in the night like a beacon of hope. Jimmy's house. "Fuck yeah! Longest quarter mile I've ever wal-ke-d. Oh fuck!" The stain on his ass grew larger as his brown-eyed poo faucet continued to spew mist. "Jesus! On-ly a f-ew more ste-p-s!"

In a wild leap, Franklin thrust himself up the steps and against the door. He dropped his pants and doubled over, a slur of loud grunts and moans spilling from his mouth as he released a spicy mist of chocolate-colored sewage. "Fuck! Yeeeeaaaaaahhhhh!" With each grunt, air exited his shitter with a force rivaling that of a hurricane. "Goddammmmmnnnnnnn!"

Squatted down and facing the street, Frankin heard the front door open behind him.

"What the fuck?" a strong voice protested.

Too deep into the orgasmic pleasure of emptying his bowels, the scenario didn't register with Franklin right away. "Ahhhh yeahhhh!" he moaned, as his flatulence continued to splatter mist all over the front porch.

"Franklin?" Jimmy looked down at him in disbelief.

Franklin was still mid-squat directly in front of him, a steady stream of ass juice flowing at his feet.

"What the fuck is going on?" He scanned the floor, now nothing more than a thick layer of brown sludge. "Are you...are you *shitting* on my porch? I'm gonna fuckin' kill you!"

Franklin continued to push, the force distending his rectum, puckering from his ass like a set of thick and juicy mud-covered lips. "Here it comes!" Like giving birth to a twelve-pound child, he pushed one final time. A turd the size of a football ejected from his now swollen and bleeding asshole sending splashes of the mess up onto Jimmy's legs.

"Holy shit! That's fucking disgusting," Jimmy yelled.

Finally able to concentrate on something other than his contractions, Franklin turned around, sweat dripping from his forehead, his eyes drooping in an exhausted and worn gaze. With tired breath, he looked at Jimmy and recited the line exactly as Fecesnura had written. "Eat my shit, Jimmy McCloud, and lick its crumbs from your lips."

"Oh, you're a dead man walkin', buddy."

Franklin's eyes widened and he stumbled backward, slipping in his own poopy slime. "B...but you're supposed to eat it! That's all the note said to do! I did everything right! Exactly as he wrote it!"

Jimmy moved onto the porch, navigating around the nastiness as best he could. "Is that right?" He bent over and grasped Franklin's collar, pulling him up to a standing position. "I told you what would happen. Remember?"

Franklin squinted, bracing himself for the worst. "But it was supposed to work!"

Jimmy drew his fist back, zeroing in on Franklin's face, but before he could unload, a noise from behind them caught his attention. It was a gulping sound, like someone drowning in the shitty pool or choking on the partial chunks left in it. Curious, he threw Franklin to the ground and spun around. "Goddamn, son! What did you shit out?"

The massive turd was moving. It wiggled around at first, from side to side like a snake. The gurgling sound grew stronger, bubbles forming in the liquid around one of its edges. The thing began to shake violently as if seizing, until large chunks of partially digested material ripped from each of its sides to take shape as legs and arms.

Both boys stood, staring at the unbelievably large shit log rolling and thrashing around in the lake of poo.

"Is it *alive?*" Jimmy muttered.

Franklin was quiet and motionless beside him. He had no idea what was happening either.

Jimmy elbowed his nemesis. "Hey, I asked you a question fuckface. What the fuck is that thing?"

"I...I'm not really sure."

In one smooth action, the turd rolled completely over and rose to a seated position. It had eyes and a mouth carved into its brown lumpy face, and it raised one arm and pointed at Jimmy. "Eat his *shit,*" it hissed. Although there were no fingers, its stubs were tipped in long polished, and pointed claws. Uneven chunks of randomly placed hair covered its head.

"Holy Hell. It's *my* hair." Franklin said. The realization shocked him. He knew what the thing was now. It was a demon, summoned from the depths of Hell to exact *his* revenge. It wasn't there for him. It was there for Jimmy.

It jumped to its feet and lunged at the bully, forcing its way into his mouth.

"Fu-ck! H-hel—" Jimmy muttered, choking on the large animated turd. Grasping his throat, he staggered around as he tried to fight the beast, only to slip on the assbile-soaked floor. As he lay there, he looked to Franklin, his eyes begging for help.

The thing worked its way into his throat and down his esophagus. His neck bulged and stretched with each inch the demon gained. From his chest cavity, one of its claws protruded, slicing him open down to his groin. Blood and organs spilled over the porch in a great wave like something you'd see in an old B-rated horror movie. It mixed with the liquid shit, rushing over Franklin's feet and over his shoes.

The demon turd leaped from Jimmy's now lifeless body, grinned at Franklin, took a bow, and fell apart into the bodily fluids from which it came.

Speechless, Franklin fell to his ass. He was trembling, partially from disbelief and partially because he knew that he was responsible for a murder now. Maybe not directly, but he'd most definitely been at least a partial cause. His DNA was everywhere. The police would certainly come looking for him. What would he say? Technically, *he* hadn't killed anyone. But how would he explain it?

"What am I supposed to—"

"Don't worry," a familiar voice said. "I'll take care of it...for the right price, that is."

He looked up and saw Fecesnura hovering in the air above him. "What do you mean?" Franklin said. "How will you do that?"

"Would you like to make another deal?"

"What? Another...what *kind* of deal?"

Fecesnura floated closer to the boy. "A very *good* deal. You give me another soul, and I'll clean the evidence away. All ties to you will be forgotten. It'll be as if they'd never existed."

"Another soul? Not *my* soul!"

"No," Fecesnura replied. "I need another *rotten* soul, remember?"

"Who?"

The corners of Fecesnura's lips curled into an evil grin. "Rossssse," he hissed. "Feed her to me and you'll be free."

Franklin sat there, studying the little demon, the situation as a whole. He knew if he did nothing, he'd be done. He'd spend the rest of his life in jail, followed by an eternity with his new friend, vomiting endlessly from his disgusting stench. "But, I can't. Not Rose."

"Then I guess I'll have to settle for you. Not my preference, but in tough times one takes what one can get."

"Wait," Franklin said. "If I take you to Rose, what happens then? Will I be linked to that murder?"

"Oh, I'm sure by then we will be able to make one *final* deal. One to clean everything up quite nicely."

Somewhere deep down, Franklin still had feelings for Rose, but he couldn't go out like this. And besides, she was part of the whole damn thing; part of the whole reason he'd gotten into this mess in the first place. "Fuck," Franklin said. "I guess you leave me with no choice. Sure. What's one more, right?"

"Exactly," Fecesnura laughed, "what's *one* more?"

END

Voodou Lemonade

By: Michael Allen Rose

April squinted up at the sun. She moved her dolly. She knew that the little plastic arms and legs would melt if they sat too long under the bright sunshine pounding down on Oak Street, and she needed to protect it from such a fate. It was special.

She watched the ice begin to melt in the two pitchers of lemonade before her. One was nearly full, but the other had almost emptied as the noonday sun beat down and people saw her hand-decorated lemonade stand. She had set up on the corner, where sidewalks intersected, and a wide parking lane on her busy residential street meant that drivers were pulling over regularly, trying to beat the heat. Commuters were like dying men seeing an oasis in the desert on a day like today when air-conditioners running at full tilt caused brownouts all across the county.

"Morning, April." It was the postman, also known as "Mailman Bob," or sometimes "Postal Service Delivery Worker Robert Paul McCain," when formally addressed.

"Hi, Mailman Bob," April chimed. "Lemonade?"

Mailman Bob pulled two quarters from his deep, blue pants pocket, and slapped them down on the little cardboard countertop. "Set me up with a glass."

April carefully removed one of the small, paper cups from its plastic sleeve. She set it on the counter, and using both hands delicately filled the cup with lemonade. She allowed one cube of ice to slide down the curve of the pitcher and it plopped into the cup with a controlled splash. Her smile beamed up at Mailman Bob as she pushed the cool drink across the "bar" to her thirsty patron.

"How's business?" asked Mailman Bob.

"Okay," said April, as she situated the pitcher back in its original ring of condensation. "But nice people have been stopping by. Some even get out of their cars. One man bought glasses for every person in his car, and they were on their way to work."

"That's good." Mailman Bob shuffled through the envelopes in his satchel.

"Any mail for me?" asked April.

Mailman Bob separated the letters and bills for her parents from a yellow, padded envelope, with a rectangular bulge. "Looks like another book for you, April." He smiled as he handed her the package. "You sure do read a lot of books. Feels like every week, I'm bringing you a new one."

"Yup!" exclaimed April, as she looked the package over.

"What kind of books do you like to read?"

"Lots of different stuff. I like learning."

"Education is important," chuckled Mailman Bob. "Are you learning how to cook? Or write screenplays? Are you going to learn how to design clothes for your dolls?"

With eyes that were far older than the little body they were attached to, April looked up at

Mailman Bob with a zen-like chilliness. "Something like that."

The postman walked up to the front door, whistling. He would have dropped the mail off with little April, but he wouldn't want an accidental lemonade spill to ruin the mail. Better to drop it through the slot. He liked having a friendly relationship with the people along his route though and loved it when he could hand kids their mail directly. He loved the smiles.

In the time that it took Mailman Bob to deliver the home's bounty of mail, April had opened her package and was rifling through the pages of a purple-covered book with lots of text. He was a little surprised to see that there were no pictures. April must be reading at quite an advanced level. As he passed by her stand, he gave her a little wave and walked next door to the Smith residence. He had to sidle out of the way of an oncoming bicycle and grimaced as Tommy Spinks pedaled by in the middle of the sidewalk without detouring.

Tommy skidded to a halt a few feet away from April's lemonade stand. "Hey, give me some lemonade."

"Do you have fifty cents?" April asked, not looking up from her book.

April knew Tommy Spinks and could draw several conclusions without knowing for sure. One was that Tommy Spinks probably didn't have any money unless he'd robbed another lemonade stand on the way over here. Two, even if he did, he would lie and say he didn't, because he was the kind of person who took things without asking and was generally kind of a shit.

"No," said Tommy. "Give me some."

"That's not how commerce works, Tommy Spinks."

"Whatever. Lemonade stands are stupid. What are you, five?"

"I'm six," said April, matter-of-factly.

Tommy frowned. He could just take the lemonade. He was two years older than this little girl, and he had muscles, and a getaway bike. But, he considered, what if an adult saw? He didn't care about his reputation, but they might get him in trouble. Tommy Spinks hated being in trouble almost as much as he hated people not giving him the things he wanted. He watched as a couple, taking a walk, crossed the street and then approached April. They were a young couple, casual and smiling. The woman approached the stand and held out a dollar bill.

"Two, please."

April slid her book under the stand's counter and smiled brightly. She poured two glasses for the couple and waited to see the results. They toasted, clinking their paper cups together, and made exaggerated "Mmmmmm" noises.

"My compliments to the sommelier," the man said.

"What's a sommelier?" Tommy asked, from his perch nearby.

"Someone who helps you find the best things to drink," April said, quietly.

"Very good, young lady!" said the man, as he grabbed his partner's hand, and they continued their walk.

Tommy stewed for a moment, watching the adults leave, as April went back to her book. "You think you're so smart. Well, you're not."

"Meh." April ran her fingers over a paragraph about halfway through her new book. She looked back and forth between it, and Tommy, who had now parked with his kickstand and was getting off his bike. She nodded, and smiled, letting the book fall closed.

Mailman Bob watched, as he finished delivering mail to the Smith house. He had plenty of distance to go, but he wanted to make sure April was okay before he continued his rounds. Tommy seemed to be menacing her. He had to admire the little girl for not backing down in the face of Tommy's physical superiority.

"Go away, Tommy. Unless you're buying lemonade." She had run into Tommy Spinks before, numerous times. He was not exactly her neighborhood bully, per se, but certainly, the kind of character she'd prefer to steer clear of. Once, he had caught her playing with her dolls on the park's playground, and when no adults were looking, had proceeded to steal two of them and bury them in the sandbox. The whole time, he was loudly saying things like "Oh, we'll miss her so much now that she's dead," and "My condolences for your loss, they died in a horrible quicksand accident and got eaten by sandworms." She had to use the little cranes to dig them back up, and when she did, their clothes were a mess.

Another time, on Halloween, she and her friends were trick-or-treating, and Tommy came by with his friends making fun of their costumes.

She had been the bravest and told Tommy to ride away or else. He had stood up to her vague threats, ridden by on his bike, and knocked her candy bag out of her hands and into a puddle. He and his little gang rode off into the evening, celebrating their delinquency. At the end of the night, taking stock of her treasure, she found that some of the hard candies, being so susceptible to moisture damage, were unsalvageable. She had told her parents about the event, who talked to Tommy's parents, and therefore got him in trouble, but that had only granted her a temporary reprieve. Soon, the boy's confidence had returned, but now with a crafty scouting procedure that made sure adults were never looking in his direction when he did his dirty deeds.

Tommy was thinking about their history as well. Mostly, he reveled in it. He thought about grabbing the lemonade pitcher, but the postman was still nearby, and walking slowly. Maybe he could make his theft look like a children's game, or just a joke. He wasn't even that thirsty, but he couldn't let some little kid tell him what he could or couldn't do. It was the principle of the thing.

Reaching for the pitcher, Tommy felt April's tiny hand on his arm.

"I'm warning you, Tommy Spinks. Be nice, or else."

There was that phrase again. "Or else? Or else what? You going to tell your mommy?"

"Nope." April took her hand off Tommy's arm and lowered it underneath her counter. It reemerged clutching her dolly. She idly played with it, shifting its little clothes.

Tommy took advantage of the momentary distraction and picked up the pitcher. He immediately tilted it back and chugged several mouthfuls of lemonade. When he glanced down at the sour look April was giving him, he snorted, and as he did so, some of the drink erupted into the back of his nasal cavity. Tommy coughed, dropping the pitcher, which bounced as the upper portion shattered, sending glass shards all over the sidewalk, and spilling the yellow liquid across the concrete and a few unfortunate anthills.

"Sorry," Tommy muttered, an insincere smirk on his face. He coughed again. "It went up my nose."

Hearing the glass shatter startled Mailman Bob. He squinted in the sunlight, wondering if he should step in. He didn't want the boy to hurt April and felt like it was his duty as the only adult present to ensure that nobody got injured.

He took one step back toward April's house, but then stood and watched as April looked at Tommy and raised her dolly up in front of her like a crucifix, aligning its silhouette with the boy. He could see the cover of the book now. It appeared to have a photograph of a circle of bones, with a deer skull in the center. Mature reading for a six-year-old.

"I warned you, Tommy Spinks," said April, as she held the doll in her right hand, and with her left, bent the right arm of the doll sharply. Tommy fell on his butt like he'd been shot.

"Ow! My arm!" he cried. A new elbow had appeared on his arm, facing in the wrong direction. April twisted and bent the arm back and forth a few times, as Tommy's own arm mirrored the doll's, cracking over and over until a bone jutted out from his upper arm, piercing the skin where his joints met.

Tommy tried to stand up and went for his bike, crying salty tears, and blubbering about how he'd be back to burn down her lemonade stand, or some such gibberish. April calmly flew the doll through the air and then bent, raking the doll's front side along the ground. As she did so, Tommy was lifted off his feet and thrown to the pavement. His body dragged forward, through the shards of splintered glass, and he howled even louder as the lemon juice worked its way into his lacerations.

The doll then abruptly changed direction, as April scraped it through the grass. Tommy followed suit, jerked to the right, and through the lemon-soaked anthills. He opened his mouth to cry out, but any sound was immediately muffled by chunks of dirt and ants piling past his gums and teeth. April let the doll come to a stop, letting Tommy rest long enough to catch his breath, spitting out filth, as he frantically flailed his broken arm and screamed.

"They're biting me!"

April lifted the doll and plunged it headfirst into the other, still full pitcher of lemonade. Tommy's body was somersaulted upside down, and his cheeks ballooned up as he struggled to breathe. Lemonade stung his eyes evoking a brilliant red as he tried to blink them clear, but the mud and blood coating his face like a death mask made it difficult to see what was happening.

April calmly walked over to Tommy's bike, still parked where he'd left it. She had learned to ride a bike the previous summer, and although she was still a little shaky, especially on a bicycle this big, she was a big, brave girl, and would risk falling off for what came next. Carefully, she walked the bike those few steps over to her lemonade stand. Tommy was choking on the ground, and beginning to turn a variety of rainbow colors. She waited until his puffy eyes looked up at her, then jerked the doll free of the pitcher, sending ice flying.

Tommy gasped on the ground, trying to idly brush off the now severely irritated ants with his working arm, sobbing and mumbling "sorry" over and over again. April smiled and gingerly placed the doll underneath the fork of the bicycle's front wheel between the spokes, like a deck of cards. She climbed onto the bicycle and slowly pushed off. Her mother would be mad that she wasn't wearing her helmet, but she figured that she wasn't going very far. Just up and down the sidewalk. She wasn't even going to cross the street.

She heard the metal spokes ping off the plastic doll's legs and torso as she picked up speed, at first, slowly, and then with sudden vibrant impacts. At the end of the block, she turned the bike around and rode back. Tommy was now a whimpering mess, covered in cuts and bruises. His clothing was torn to shreds, and snot flowed from his broken nose like lava from an active volcano.

April stood, looking down at Tommy. She thought about all the books she'd been reading, preparing for this day. That day at school lunch when Tommy had thought it would be hilarious to take some of his hair and put it in her sandwich when she went to get more milk, well, that wasn't the first day she'd begun looking up books on metaphysics, voodou, occultism, and chaos magick, but she'd certainly become a more voracious reader since then. She idly pet the doll's head, which contained a carefully trimmed chunk of the very hair that Tommy had put between her tomatoes and her cheese.

Tommy looked up at April, as the little girl grasped the doll's head between her thumb and pointer finger. She tugged slightly on its neck, and Tommy felt his throat muscles stretch and burn with tension. "No, no, please! I'm sorry!" He was bawling now, his speech practically indecipherable. It looked as though with very little additional force; it would pop clean off.

April smiled and walked back to her stand, where she carefully tucked the doll in with a napkin, like a tiny doll bed, and placed it gently under the counter. "See you later, Tommy. You should be more careful when you ride your bike."

Tommy couldn't ride a bike, in his condition, but he was able to shamble home, all the while trying to think of the best story he could about falling down a hill on his bicycle to tell his parents as they took him to the emergency room.

April walked into her house and closed the door. When she came back out, she had a roll of paper towels and diligently cleaned up the spilled glass as best she could. She went back in and came back out a few minutes later with a fresh pitcher of lemonade, this one, plastic.

She looked around to see if any new customers were coming. All she saw was Mailman Bob, who stood, frozen, his jaw dropped low, and his little mustache twitching. She removed another little cup from its plastic sleeve, and set it atop her brand-new copy of The Clavicule of Solomon (with commentary from Honorius of Thebes), pouring carefully until it was nearly full.

April walked the lemonade over to Mailman Bob, who took the cup with shaking hands. "This one is my treat," said the little girl. Her little yellow dress reflected the sunlight and made her face shine like an angel's wing. "Did you see Tommy fall off his bike?"

Mailman Bob exhaled. His mouth was dry. He didn't know how long he'd been holding his breath. "I did. Yes. Thank… thank you. April." he managed to stammer.

"Maybe if he was nicer to people, like you, bad stuff wouldn't happen to him. Oh well."

As the little girl went back to her lemonade stand, another car was already stopping against the curb. Some guys in baseball uniforms got out, and grinned, as April went into her sales pitch, smiling like only a sweet little girl can. The men were already reaching for their wallets as they unthinkingly stepped over the reddish-brown stains next to the sidewalk.

Mailman Bob pulled a tiny airplane bottle of vodka from his zipper pocket, and trembling, poured it into the lemonade cup, then went back to completing his rounds.

Something Is A--Uh-- Without Feet--At the Circle S

By: Nikolas P. Robinson

"You have to pay for that, Jimmy." Sam rolled his eyes as his best friend snagged an hours-old, wrinkling hotdog from the rollers and slid it into the stale bun before fishing some condiments from the containers. If the two of them hadn't gotten stoned a few minutes before, even Jimmy wouldn't have been eying the questionable food the way he was. Cast iron stomach or not, everyone had limits, and the meat Jimmy had just snagged for a meal was something likely to push anyone beyond those limits.

"Pay for this?" Jimmy raised the unappetizing snack as if Sam needed to see it more clearly to know the quality of the meal. "You have to be fucking kidding me."

"You eat here for free all the damn time."

"This," Jimmy said, raising the mummified stick of meat to his nostrils, "is not food. It's probably not even edible."

"Then don't eat it. Throw it the fuck away." Sam attempted to stifle a laugh. "But if you eat the fucking thing, you're paying for it."

The exaggerated huff from Jimmy was the final straw for Sam, and his laughter spilled out like sewage from the overflowing toilet he had to contend with almost nightly while he was working.

Jimmy grinned and took a bite of the offensive meat byproduct, chewing more than one should have to, before reluctantly swallowing his first mouthful of a meal he knew he'd later regret.

Sam's laughter immediately ceased. "You're still paying for that."

"Fuck you!"

The two young men both smiled and Jimmy tossed the remains of the hot dog into the garbage before turning to the soda machine to find something he could use to wash the taste out of his mouth.

"You're paying for that too," Sam chided. Of course, he knew Jimmy wouldn't be paying for anything. He never did, and Sam never tried to enforce the rule. He played this game with Jimmy once in a while to get him riled up and pass the time.

Sam knew if it went like any other night, they'd end up scratching a handful of lottery tickets until they won enough to pay for the ones they'd scratched off already. Sometimes they'd get lucky and come out ahead by a few bucks, but they never wound up with the windfall of a few thousand dollars they always hoped to discover. They were just lucky enough that neither Sam nor Jimmy had to pay anything out-of-pocket to cover the scratchers they went through.

But it wasn't like any other night.

It was distinctly not a dark and stormy night outside, with no flashes of lightning adding dramatic flair and no rumbling thunder shaking the building. It was warm and humid well past dusk, and there was no sign that the rest of the night would cool down sufficiently to erase that muggy quality of everything.

Unfortunately, the convenience store's AC was barely functional, and the repair wasn't scheduled for another couple of days. Sam normally tried to keep the place barely a stone's throw from the interior of an icebox, but not that night. That night, the thick air that clung to everything had made its way inside and coated both he and Jimmy with what felt like oil or grease.

When the door came crashing open, causing the electronic alarm to produce its annoying doorbell ding-dong impression, neither Sam nor Jimmy was prepared to see the disheveled young woman stumbling into the store's interior, breathing heavily and covered in sweat.

She looked around frantically, taking in her surroundings, panic in her eyes.

Her eyes landed on Sam in his wrinkled uniform shirt. "You've got to help!"

"Sure," he said, taken aback by her appearance as much as her presence. "What can I do for you? Are you okay?"

She bent over at the waist, placing her palms on her thighs just above the knees, struggling to get her breathing under control. When she stood straight again, she wasn't quite on the verge of hyperventilation anymore, but she still appeared just as close to outright terror as when she'd burst through the door. "They're after me," she said. "These men—monsters—whatever the hell they are."

Jimmy grinned, figuring this was some stupid prank being pulled on them, or maybe something Sam had arranged just to fuck with him. "Man-monsters are coming after you?"

He glanced at Sam out of the corner of his eye, looking for the telltale signs that his friend had orchestrated this, but Sam looked just as confused and nervously amused as Jimmy was feeling.

"Yeah," Sam said, "I think we're gonna need a bit of context here. Who exactly is after you? Also—why is anyone after you?"

"I'm going to sound crazy." She shook her head, a defeated look replacing some of the fear in her expression. "They're—like—weresnakes."

Sam remained silent for a moment, his brain struggling to catch up after hearing what she'd said. "Wait a second," he said after a few seconds. "Did you say weresnakes? Like werewolves? I'm not sure I heard you right."

"Buddy, you heard her right," Jimmy said, the exertion required to hold back his laughter raising the pitch of his voice. "She said weresnakes. You know, like the bad guy James Earl Jones played in Conan."

He barely got the words out before erupting in laughter, certain now that someone was fucking with them for some reason or that the girl was on drugs, he hoped he could manage to avoid for his own well-being. Sam smirked and began to shake with silent laughter himself.

"It's not a joke!" The girl's attitude shifted entirely, and she no longer displayed any fear or uncertainty. She was angry and frustrated, and the sincerity in her tone and expression left Sam and Jimmy both concerned that they were dealing with a total headcase or a drug addict that might be a threat if they didn't play their cards right in dealing with her.

Cowed by the outburst, neither of the two young men knew what to say or do.

"This is real," the girl continued, breaking the tense silence. "I don't know what they are, but weresnakes was the only thing I could think to call them. They're men who turn into snakes, so what the fuck else would I call them? What would you call that?"

"Do they turn into a single large snake, or do they transform into a bunch of smaller snakes?" Jimmy paused for a second, his face screwed up in concentration. "What the fuck do we call a bunch of snakes together? Calling them a herd of snakes just sounds stupid. A flock of snakes doesn't sound any better."

"A swarm," Sam offered.

Jimmy nodded his head excitedly. "Yes! A swarm of snakes!"

The girl shook her head, confused and disheartened by the reaction from the two young men. But her terror wasn't buried deep, and she started to cry. They were silent sobs of resignation. There was none of the help she'd hoped to find when she saw the convenience store lights slicing through the muggy night. No one had called the police. No one had attempted to offer her comfort, and neither of the two men she'd been confronted with seemed to be capable of helping her in any way, nonetheless saving her.

Sam wasn't a stupid man, and he could read all of that in the distraught girl's pained expression, a mélange of fear, disappointment, and regret. He may not have been able to discern her precise thoughts, but he could suss out enough of an approximation that he was near enough to the mark.

"Shit," he said. "I'm sorry. What's your name, lady?"

"Excuse me?" She shook her head rapidly. "What? What fucking relevance is that?" The look in her eyes was enough to take both Sam and Jimmy by surprise.

Sam shrugged and took an involuntary step backward, slightly raising his hands before noticing what he was doing and returning them to his side.

Jimmy's face turned red, whether from embarrassment or frustration, he wouldn't have been able to say, since he felt both things in approximately equal measure. He reflexively wanted to defend his best friend but didn't know enough about what was going on to insert himself between his friend and this psychotic newcomer.

The rage in her expression deflated as she noticed the reactions from the two of them. She sighed, glanced behind her through the glass of the entrance, and then said, "My name's Maggie."

Forcing a smile onto his face, Sam introduced himself as pleasantly as he could, hoping to diffuse any further angry outbursts.

"Jimmy," was all Jimmy said when Sam finished, less inclined to be polite and civil with the girl who was ruining their night. He could tell already that things were going to get worse before they got better, and he didn't like anything about the situation with this crazy lady who had burst in on them and added tension and confusion to what should've been a relaxed night hanging out at the store.

"So," Sam began, "what is with these weresnakes? Why are they after you?"

"And are they venomous?" Jimmy blurted out the question without any pause, barely allowing Sam time to finish his inquiry.

"I don't know why they're after me," Maggie said. "I don't know whether they're venomous. I don't know anything about them. I didn't know they existed until tonight."

Sam stifled a reflexive chuckle. "Fuck you and your ADHD, Jimmy. Do we need to know if they're venomous?"

Jimmy applied a familiar sulking expression before replying. "I don't know. What if they can spit, like a cobra?"

"I don't think cobras actually do that," Sam said. "I think that's just something from movies, like quicksand and piranhas being man-eaters."

"What the fuck're you talking about? Quicksand is real."

"No, it's—"

"What the fuck is wrong with you two?" Maggie's voice carried the resonance of a barely contained scream and wholly uncontained scorn.

"Fuck, I'm sorry," Sam said.

"Me too," Jimmy added.

Maggie glanced back and forth between the two of them for a few seconds. To Sam, she appeared to be struggling to decide whether there was any point in staying here when she could've continued running.

"I'm sorry," she finally said. Consciously breathing deep and even, she got her panic under control. "I'm under a lot of stress and I'm terrified right now. It's not your fault, and I've laid a lot on you tonight."

"It's ok," Sam said.

"Also, cobras do spit venom," she said. "And quicksand isn't real, not like you see it in movies and cartoons, at least."

"So..." Jimmy started to speak.

"I don't fucking know if they spit venom, or if they're venomous at all," Maggie said, losing some of the self-control she'd struggled to manifest.

"Sorry," Jimmy said, his shoulders slumping in response to the chastisement.

"Can we call someone for you?" Sam pulled his cell phone from his pocket. "I can't believe we didn't think to do that already."

"Who are we supposed to call?" Maggie asked.

"The police, the Sheriff—animal control?" Jimmy suggested.

Sam glared at his friend, recognizing that if they started making jokes or treating the situation as one, the girl was going to lose her shit all over again, and he didn't want that. It wasn't just because she was pretty, in that manic, mortified way a final girl might be in a movie—but she was that. It was more a matter of Sam wanting to do the right thing, whatever that might be, under such peculiar circumstances.

"Sorry," Jimmy mumbled.

"What am I supposed to tell the police?" Maggie asked. "I'm being chased by snake people, or weresnakes, or whatever the fuck we'd call them? I'm sure that would go over smoothly with anyone who answered the phone. They totally wouldn't just hang up on me immediately and dismiss it as a prank call."

"Maybe they know about these things?"

Jimmy suggested.

"He's right," Sam said. "Maybe you're not the first person to run into these people, or whatever the fuck they are."

"Just because we've never heard of them doesn't mean they aren't known in these parts," Jimmy said.

"Yeah," Sam agreed. "We're not exactly the most with-it where local superstitions and legends are concerned."

"Maybe you're right," Maggie said, the words almost coming out as a question. "Maybe we should just dial 9-1-1 and see what happens."

"We don't even need to mention the snake thing," Sam said. "We could just say that you were being chased through the woods by some guys who wanted to hurt you."

Maggie stood rigid for a couple of seconds before letting out a deep breath that terminated in quiet sobs. Tears started to build up in her eyes and she smiled ever so slightly. As she controlled her breathing, she said, "Thank you two so much."

"No problem," Sam said as he unlocked his screen and dialed 9-1-1.

Telling the operator where they were located and that a girl had come running into the store while being chased by bad guys wasn't too time-consuming and the operator kept Sam on the line, advising him that they'd be sending an officer.

"So," Jimmy said, "I've got to ask. Do they have like human legs, arms, and whatnot, but with a snake head jutting out from the top?"

"Like that movie Dreamscape," Sam muttered,

after covering the phone's microphone.

"Yeah, those things always creeped me the hell out," Jimmy said.

"Spooked me out too," Sam said.

"You ever see that movie?" Jimmy asked. "Dennis Quaid, I think it was."

"And the weird little guy who played T-Bird in The Crow."

"Plus Max von Sydow," Jimmy added.

"Oh yeah," Sam said. "I forgot he was in that one too. What a great flick."

"So," Jimmy turned to look at Maggie, "have you seen that one?" If he'd been blessed with just a bit more empathy, he might have halted before finishing the question, but Jimmy was stoned and amped up from the previous minutes' events, and he wasn't capable of thinking things through.

She stared at them, her mouth open in stunned silence, unsure how to react. At that moment it was clear to even Jimmy that she was sure she'd made a huge mistake coming through the door to that particular convenience store. She was desperate for help of some kind, but there wasn't any help to be found with the two young men she was quickly coming to loathe.

"Fuck you guys," Maggie said.

She turned away from them and stormed back to the door she'd come through only minutes earlier. "I'll take my chances out there."

"But the cops are on their way," Sam protested as Maggie shoved the door open, producing another wheezing ding from the alarm as she passed through the exit and back to the sidewalk outside.

Through the window, Sam and Jimmy both

watched her as she checked her surroundings, stunned that she'd actually left the way she had. Looking confident that she knew where to go, she turned to her left and began a slow jog toward the edge of the building facing the main road.

Sam returned the phone to his ear and said, "Yeah, the girl who was here—she just took off."

He described her to the dispatcher, recalling her clothing as best he could, and the voice at the other end of the line assured him the officer would look for her when he got closer.

Sam disconnected the call and let his hand fall to his side.

The two of them just watched the empty parking lot, lit by the sodium lamps. Losing track of time, they had no idea how much time passed before they heard the high-pitched scream that could be mistaken for nothing but abject terror. They both recognized the voice, even though it was so thoroughly outside of the register they'd heard before as to be virtually alien from the panicked young woman they'd been talking to only minutes before.

The first scream was followed by another, more drawn-out screech of agony that died on the lips of the girl they knew had also died.

Sam shivered in the uncomfortably warm and stagnant air with a chill that had nothing to do with the night air or the malfunctioning air conditioning in the store.

"Well," Jimmy said, "That's fucked."

Sam thought for a moment before replying. "Someone really was after her, I suppose." He paused for a few seconds. "I sort of figured she was just tripping balls or mentally ill."

"Could still be one or both?" Jimmy shrugged. His attempt at levity failed before it even started. There was no humor in his eyes when Sam turned to look at him. Those screams had guaranteed as much.

The look of weary resignation and failure transformed in an instant. Sadness was replaced by terror, as Jimmy caught sight of something from the corner of his eye, just beyond the edge of the cone of light from the lamp nearest the perpetually empty road with the pretense of being called a country highway that passed by the convenience store.

Sam turned to look for himself, unsure if he wanted to see whatever it might be that had his best friend looking horrified.

It took a few seconds of concentration, but in the shadows just past the illusion of safety afforded by the light, something appeared to be moving. The specifics were challenging to pinpoint, but Sam was certain the best word he could use to describe what he was seeing was that it was something slithering. And it wasn't anything small.

"Hey," Sam said, backing slowly away from the large windows at the front of the store. "Let's go check on the cooler and get some cool air in the process."

"Good thinking," Jimmy said, backing away as well.

The two of them made their way as quickly as they could—without looking like they were scared—to the employee-only door at the rear of the store. From there, they made their way into the refrigerated air of the cooler. Sam positioned himself so that he could see past the rows of canned and bottled soft drinks to the front door and the parking lot immediately beyond, not wanting to see anything at all, but knowing that he had to.

Nothing happened.

No slithering monstrosity slammed itself against the door or windows, though both Sam and Jimmy were anticipating precisely that sort of thing happening.

The hissing of an air compressor kicking on made both of them jump, even though the sound of that particular piece of equipment was so familiar to Sam that he wouldn't have noticed it under any other circumstances.

They passed the time with idle chit-chat and pointless speculation about a number of topics that had nothing at all to do with herpetology. Neither of them knew the word herpetology, and if they'd heard someone use it, they'd have both assumed it had something to do with herpes— what Jimmy often referred to as the Greek God of Surprise.

A couple of hours passed in the chill air of the refrigerated compartment, and both Sam and Jimmy were shivering by the time they decided it might be safe to leave the relative safety and security of the cold.

"So," Jimmy said as they made their way to the front door, "that was weird."

Sam nodded his head.

The artificial bell-like ding of the alarm startled them both as they stepped outside into the still night air.

They scanned their surroundings, searching

for any details that stood out as unusual and seeing nothing alarming.

"Let's circle around the building and check things out," Sam said, attempting to display bravery he didn't feel at all.

"Sure," Jimmy replied uncertainly.

Following the same path Maggie had when she left the building, they saw nothing out of the ordinary on that side of the building. The rear employee parking area that played host to the dumpster and utility hook-ups brought them no surprises either.

It was only when they had almost completed their circuit of the building that Jimmy noticed something shimmery near the edge of the parking area.

"What's that?"

Sam squinted his eyes in a futile attempt to pick out what his friend had seen. "No idea."

Without saying a word, they both began walking toward what appeared to be some sort of semi-transparent plastic used on construction sites.

As they got closer, both of them felt a new chill traversing their spines, just as contrary to the warm, muggy air as before.

"Well, that answers one question," Jimmy said, turning to look at Sam.

"Yeah, definitely the Conan the Barbarian sort of weresnakes."

As the discarded layer of scaled skin rustled in the barely existent breeze, both young men turned and headed back to the front door. Jimmy fished a joint out of his pocket, lit it with the lighter Sam provided, and took a hit before passing it to his friend.

"Well, that's fucked." Sam didn't know what else to say. There wasn't anything that could sum up what the two of them were feeling any better than those few words.

"I was sort of hoping for the swarm of snakes," Jimmy said. "I'd have settled for something like the snake people from Dreamscape too."

Sam nodded. He took a hit and passed the joint back to Jimmy.

"Cops never showed up," Jimmy said.

"Yeah. You suppose they found Maggie?"

Jimmy shook his head. "I figure she was swallowed whole like a mouse or something."

"Probably," Sam said, noticing for the first time—but not drawing attention to—the strange markings in the gravel at the edge of the parking lot. Marks that looked an awful lot like the trail left behind by a few snakes slithering through the loosely packed surface. Jimmy had seen them as well but was invested in pretending he hadn't.

"Weresnakes?" Jimmy finally said after exhaling the smoke from his last hit from the joint.

"I guess so," Sam said.

"Fuck," Jimmy said.

Sam nodded in response as he reached for the door and a return to the normal world without things like weresnakes to worry about. He wasn't sure how successful he'd be, but he was damn well going to try.

* * *

The Assassination of Mr. Baltisberger

By: John Baltisberger

1

The cigar smoke hung heavy in the air like a funerary censor. It filled the room, creating a haze that would be difficult for anyone to see through even if the lighting was adequate. It was not. The bare concrete room was lit by a single bare bulk that hung from the ceiling like a melancholic billionaire in a jail cell. Its harsh, unforgiving light did its best to cut through the heavy smoke of the room but did little to truly illuminate the scene. What it did shine a light on, however, was nothing that anybody wanted to see.

Tim Murr sat on a wooden stool, just outside the pool of light under the bulb. He examined his cigar, little more than a cherry smoldering in a paper nub at this point. It had been a long day. A long, exhausting day. His knuckles hurt, and he was tired. But you didn't get where he was by being lazy. Being an indie publisher wasn't for the meek. Sure, the millions in cash, drugs, and women were perks that made the grind worth it. But there was an ugly side that these younger, more naive publishers didn't want to recognize. They didn't want to pay their dues.

Tim ground his teeth together at the thought of it. "I've been doing this shit too long to brook the disrespect from these young bloods and upstarts. It makes my fuckin' blood boil." He sighed, taking one last puff of the cigar before reaching forward, snubbing the cigar out on the bare nipple of the man in front of him. "But that isn't what we're talking about, is it, John Wayne?"

John Wayne Comunale bucked under the cruel ministrations from the larger publisher. "Man, fuck you!" he spat. A loose tooth tapped against Murr's Black Flag shirt; knocked out earlier during a round of questioning. "You're fucking crazy."

"Crazy." Tim sighed and stood, stretching his legs. He looked around the room at the others gathered just outside the reach of the bulb's kiss. As he turned back, he backhanded John Wayne with enough force to cause the chair to totter and fall to the side, knocking John Wayne's head against the cold, blood-splattered cement. "No, I'm protecting my fucking own, you prick." He stared down at the man for a second before turning away and wiping the blood off his knuckles with a silk kerchief. "Pick him up."

RJ stepped forward out of the gloom and righted the chair, pulling John Wayne up. He braced John Wayne's shoulders and looked up expectantly at Tim, but Tim didn't make a move. Instead, Tony "the Rat-Fucker" Evans stepped up to bat. He twirled the weapon in one hand, relishing the moment before he took a batter's stance and swung his first of many warm-up swings.

—

John Wayne put up a good resistance. He didn't break until Bridgette Nelson stepped up to the plate and put her nursing knowledge to work. There was only so much scrotal dissection a man could take before he gave in. Tim had stayed and watched the entire time. There was something so damn sexy about a woman in a blouse administering severe torture to another man's testes. But now he had everything he needed.

"Paul. Jeff. Get your teams ready and go. We know where Baltisberger is. We know his defenses. Fuck. Him. Up."

2

Jeff Strand glanced up from the GPS on his phone. He had a good team. Essig was a brutal author with a likewise brutal taste for violence. Nikki was a femme fatale with a knack for investigation and figuring out the clues. When hunting someone like Baltisberger, her investigative experience would give him an edge over Paul's team. Jeff smirked at that thought. They were all on the same side, of course, but everyone knew that the teams that performed were the ones who got the contracts. If Paul wanted to supplant Jeff's mastery of horror comedy, he would need to have a better squad, perform better hits, *be better*. Jeff wasn't worried. Kenzie Jennings drove them in the sleek Lincoln Continental that she had bought with her first Splatter Western check; cool, calm, and collected, Kenzie was a hard woman. Bridgette Nelson rounded out his team, a perfect squad balanced between action and thought, movement and stillness. Brutality and thoughtful maliciousness. Casual cruelty was nothing new for the four of them; hell, they had honed it to a craft. Jeff's smirk turned into a full cruel smile as they turned the corner and began driving towards the MHP offices. This night would be bloody, bloody, and glorious.

"You think we'll have any problems?" Essig asked from the back seat.

"Problems?" Nikki asked, not taking her eyes off the road. "Problems from what? Most of MHP's posse if out of state for AuthorCon, perfect opportunity to strike."

"I'm still bummed we had to miss that," Bridget confessed.

There was a moment of silence. They were all sorry they had to miss the big gathering out east, a chance to reconnect with peers, find out who had been lost in action, or signed their souls away over the last year. But this was important. They would lose fewer authors in the future to monsters like Baltisberger if they put an end to him now.

"I heard that he signed some new heavyweights, like Wrath. I don't want to go toe-to-toe with that dude," Essig admitted.

"Wrath?" Jeff chuckled. "Don't worry, Wrath is a professional. Even if he did sign with Baltisberger, he wouldn't let that drag him down; besides, he'll probably be in Virginia just like the rest of them. We have a clear shot right now, and we're going to fucking take it."

The car jolted to a jarring halt. Jeff glared at Kenzie for the sudden stop. "What the fuck are-" was as far as he got before he looked up and saw for himself why she had stopped.

In the middle of the road, right before their car, Michael Allen Rose stood, wearing nothing but a samurai sword across his back and a bright red bow tied around the head of his cock.

"Jeff?" Kenzie asked, a tremble of fear in her normally cold voice.

The fear annoyed Jeff, not because they shouldn't be worried about Michael, he was a madman, and in the bright beams of the headlights, he looked like some sort of avenging Cossack angel.

"Fuck it," Essig grunted and kicked open the door, pulling himself out. He pulled his pistol out of its holster and held it loosely by his side. "Hey there, buddy … what are you doing?"

"Can't let you guys through; can't let you have at my friend," Michael lamented, the manic smile never leaving his face.

"Your friend?" Essig asked. "The fuck has Baltisberger ever done for you? He's nothing but a piece of shit trying to get his own slice of-" That was as far as he got as Michael taint-slid across the hood of the car, leaving a trail of glitter from his shimmering ball sack, and cut through Essig in on chop.

"Goddamn, this is a cool sword," Michael whooped. Michael refused to simply say anything. "Who else wants to take a trip to hell with him?"

"Go," Jeff commanded. His team might be scared of Michael, but they feared him more. Jeff had a reputation for being unforgiving and cruel, one that kept the others in line.

Bridget and Nikki got out of the car, each one unfolding in a beautiful display of feminine lethality. Kenzie stayed put, her fingers white on the steering wheel, betraying her frayed nerves. Perhaps watching Comunale be put down had been too much for her. Jeff also stayed seated; it wasn't worth dirtying his suit when the ladies could handle this.

Nikki didn't give Michael the same opening Essig had, raising her gun as she got clear of the car door and firing. The shot went wide, as first shots tend to. Nikki needed an editor, not for her prose but someone to proofread her firing stance. Jeff made a mental note that when they got back, he would make sure she took more classes at the range. Michael easily dodged Nikki's second shot as she panicked trying to track his movement instead of anticipating where he would be. Not a great mistake to make. Not the worst maybe, if Michael had been on the other side of the road. But he wasn't. He was right there in front of her, and the samurai sword whished through the air with Michael's stereotypical flamboyance. The red that splashed against the window was discolored by the bits of undigested corn and food bits that joined the splatter.

Nikki sunk to her knees; the copper smell of her blood, overshadowed by the reek of her perforated intestines spilling feces out onto the street. Jeff erased his mental note; Nikki wouldn't need an editor ever again. He wasn't too worried. Bridget never failed to deliver.

She pulled herself out of the car and smiled sweetly at Michael. The scalpel she held in her right hand wasn't as impressive or as intimidating as the sword Michael was gallivanting about with, but she was fucking deadly with it.

"Bridget, just go home," Michael whispered. "Just drop your knife, go home, and pet your kitties. Do you have kitties? You should have kitties. I bet Jeff Burk could get you as many kitties as you want. How many do you want, Bridget?"

"You can keep your kitties, Michael. Well, someone can; could be you, if you just turn your happy ass around and walk away," Bridget replied, never losing the sing-song quality in her voice.

"Oh, you!" Michael squealed, his smile stretching impossibly wide as he planted a foot on the side mirror, giving Jeff a full view of his glitter-covered sack and butthole, and bounded over the car at Bridget.

Bridget was not as slow to react as Essig or Nikki, though; she dodged back under the swipe of the sword and casually flicked her hand out. Blood poured down the windshield, followed by a single white grape-shaped testicle, neatly severed from its wires and sheath. Michael didn't even slow down, landing on the other side of the car in a crouch.

"I got plenty of those!" he howled, launching himself at Bridget again.

Did he? Did he have plenty of testes? And if he did, did he just mean that since he had two losing one wasn't a big deal? Maybe that isn't what he meant at all; maybe he had a bunch of them. Maybe he was just riddled with extra testicles just under the skin. Or maybe he kept a plethora of loose testes sitting around his house, popping them in his mouth to suck on like olives.

Jeff considered all the possibilities of Michael's plenty as, outside the car, Bridget and Rose battled it out. Michael was like a Kabuki actor, his movements fluid but exaggerated, giving Bridget more than enough time to see the attacks coming, get out of the way, and launch her own counterattack. It wasn't a long fight. Michael was too showy, and Bridget didn't mince words or time, only flesh. Bridget twirled under a thrust from Michael, avoiding both his blade and his seeping manhood as she slammed her scalpel into his collar and sliced up through his neck, well into his chin. She stepped back, giving Michael the room to bleed out that he would need. It was too easy. Jeff smirked as Bridget wiped the blade of her scalpel clean on her pants and stepped forward.

His smirk faded as he watched Michael Allen Rose rise back up, flesh rippling as though it was barely containing something boiling beneath the surface. The line she had sliced open was flapping, jagged white teeth emerging from the flesh seam dripping with thick blood and drool.

"Fuck." Jeff muttered, "Drive, Kenzie!"

"But what about Bri-" Kenzie protested.

"She's fucking dead already!" Jeff shouted. He wondered if Bridget's wide-eyed expression was from the fact that the door was open and she could definitely hear what he was saying, or if it was from the shock she was experiencing as Rose's newly formed vertical mouth tore her in half.

In the end, it didn't matter. Kenzie hit the gas, the car jerked forward, ramming into Rose and what was left of Bridget before Kenzie reversed, sending them flying backward down the road.

Kenzie was too busy watching the road behind them; she didn't see what Jeff saw. Michael stood still, watching them for a moment, and then, without taking a single step, reached out towards them. His arm, it wasn't even an arm anymore; it was a tentacle roiling with madness and corruption, stretched towards them, faster than should be possible, faster than they could drive. Kenzie didn't see death coming, but Jeff did, and he would be fucked sideways by Shane McKenzie if he was going to let it happen like this.

In one smooth motion, Jeff lifted his own gun and pointed it at Kenzie. She had enough time to look startled before he painted the windshield with her brains. Cruel, maybe, but far kinder than if she had seen the terrible appendage that was even now grabbing onto the bumper of the car. Jeff didn't hesitate; he placed the gun in his mouth and joined Kenzie in the Jackson Pollocking of the interior.

3

Paul Lubaczewski listened to the gunfire echoing a few blocks away, and then the screech of tires, and then something else, something terrible laughing as though at the world's greatest joke. That would be Jeff's team gone then. A great loss for comedy horror, for indie lit, but not for Paul. Now he could ascend the throne of comedy horror alone, claim all the riches and bitches that such a title afforded. He would have preferred to do it by hard work and brilliant writing, sure, but if Jeff went and got himself killed off, then that was just fine by him.

"Guess they chose the wrong path," Damien Casey said from the back seat. He sat with his eyes closed, in a meditative state, heightening his senses and reflexes so that when they ran into opposition, and they would run into opposition, he would be prepared.

"Guess so," Nikolas Robinson agreed. He was the newest to Paul's team, green, fresh. He had proven himself on the godless killing fields of extreme horror, though. He had shown that he could take things so far over the edge they circled back to funny. Paul just hoped he wouldn't get in the fucking way.

"Occupational hazard; Strand knew the stakes when he started out," Paul said, not taking his eyes off the road. "And not one that we're safe from yet. Just because they encountered resistance doesn't mean we won't. Remember, we fail as a team or we win as a team. Rising tide and all that bullshit."

Nikolas nodded. "Right, but it won't matter to him anymore if we're doing well."

"It's what he would have wanted," Paul growled. "He wouldn't want you to pussy out and stop working on writing, or on murdering Baltisberger either. Right?"

"Right," Nik said, cowed. "Who do you think they ran into?" he asked after a moment.

"Mangum would be my guess, that or Bauman's golem," Damien said.

"They have a golem?" Nik asked, surprised.

"Of course, they have a golem! Baltisberger runs that little side cabal of Jewish occultists; why wouldn't they have a golem?" Paul growled.

"What about Mangum?" Nik asked.

"Jesus, what is up with the questions, Nik? What does it matter?" Paul sighed; his nerves frayed as he tried to watch every shadow they passed.

"Mangum's an occultist too, but he also has friends, Wile, Wesley, Harding. If Mangum wants to get his hands on an arsenal, he'll get his hands on an arsenal. Jeff could have all the femme fatale assassins he wants, and it won't do shit if Mangum brings an RPG to a knife fight."

"We didn't hear any explosions, Damien," Paul said. "So it was the Golem ... probably."

"Probably," Damien agreed. Though he didn't sound half convinced.

Paul understood, these two were city-folk. They hadn't spent the time he had in the backwoods of the Everglades or the mountains. They didn't know West Bygod and its granny magic. Paul, on the other hand, was ready.

They continued to drive slowly down the empty street, each moment aching with the knowledge that at any point, they could be swarmed by whatever authors, reviewers, and artists Baltisberger had swayed over to his side during his brief rise to power. But nothing did come for them. Paul was able to pull into the empty lot in front of the Madness Heart Press corporate offices and park.

The three men got out of the car, each one acutely aware that this was all too easy. It wasn't until they pushed through the open doors that they understood why.

"Why, hello, boys." The voice was sweet, kind, and motherly. But Paul recognized it, she may be a mother, but she was definitely a mother fucker.

"Christine," Paul greeted her.

"Ms. Morgan," Nik echoed.

Damien didn't respond. He breathed slowly, reaching behind him for the collapsible baton he carried with him for violent encounters.

"Now, now," Christine chided. "Let's not be hasty. You whip that out and I'll shove it up your ass and ride out your death throes reverse cowgirl like you were a rampaging bronco."

Damien froze. She was just one woman. Sure, one woman who had Edward Lee at her back. No one wanted to fuck with Lee; you fucked with Lee; you were fucked. That was before you considered that if Morgan was here, Snyder was probably close by too. It was a trap. That's why she was here: with Christine guarding the entrance, who would dare enter?

Paul considered his options. They couldn't just leave; there was too much at stake here. Tim had made his move, and live or die, the cards had to land where they fell.

Paul raised his hands, showing that he didn't have a weapon. Somewhere in the back of his mind, he wondered if Jeff had tried to sacrifice his team to get closer, or to get away. Either way, Paul's choice was clear, he turned and tossed the loose bag of powder he had palmed into Damien's face. The powder was bright red as it exploded in his face. For a second, Damien looked surprised, but that didn't last long; it very quickly transformed into mindless rage.

"Go!" Paul turned and grabbed Nikolas by the shirt, pulling him away from Damien, who was howling now. Damien was a dead man, but the hoodoo powder that Paul had tossed would transform him into a monster, maybe even one capable of going toe-to-toe with Morgan. Paul doubted it. More likely, it would just give them time.

He rushed past Christine, who was already opening her arms to welcome an oncoming bull. Her eager expression disturbed Paul more than the murder of his friend. Too late now. He pulled Nikolas with him as he ran down the entry foyer and hit the elevators. Tense seconds passed as they listened to Christine and the maddened Damien fighting. Paul wondered how long he would last, but he didn't stick around to find out. As soon as the elevator doors opened, he jumped into the elevator and tapped the penthouse floor and the Close Door buttons.

Paul stared at the doors as they rode the elevator up, not meeting Nikolas's eyes.

"You killed him."

"I saved us," Paul snapped. "All of us, or just him. If you want to go back down there and die with him, be my fucking guest."

Nik didn't respond. They rode the rest of the way up in relative silence, the only sound being the muzak rendition of Monster Magnet songs.

The elevator doors opened up onto a lavish reception room, so brightly lit it was nearly blinding. Paul stepped forward but stopped when he saw they weren't alone. Lisa Lee Tone looked up from her computer, a bored expression of disinterest plastered across her face.

"Mr. Lubaczewski," she said before glancing at Nikolas, at least at him she had the decency to look disappointed. "Nik."

"Uh ..." Paul started, caught a little off guard by the greeting.

"Mr. Baltisberger will see you now. He's been waiting."

Behind her, as if they had a mind of their own, the doors of the office opened. Paul didn't need a better invitation than that; he and Nik passed Lisa and entered the office. He didn't wait, he didn't need to engage in banter or polite platitudes. Baltisberger died now. He raised his gun, took aim, and pulled the trigger three times.

Four gunshots rang out.

4

Tim Murr sighed, looking down at his gold-plated iPhone as it chimed. It was done. The nightmare was over. Sure some of those authors wouldn't be coming back, but that was the price of being an insanely wealthy indie horror publisher. He glanced down at the corpse of John Wayne Comunale as he began the process of lighting a fresh cigar. "Shoulda played ball, dipshit."

"Not with you." The voice echoed from all around Tim, emerging from the smoky shadow of the room.

"Baltisberger?" Tim whirled around, trying to find the source of the voice. It was definitely Baltisberger, but it was wrong, terribly wrong, discordant. "You're dead. Nik said you were dead."

"Nik is mine, Tim. He's always been mine."

The smoke was getting heavier, as though it was becoming something else, something solid. Tendrils of the haze seemed to move without any stimulus, writhing and unraveling like the tentacles of some unknowable creature. This, this is why John Baltisberger needed to die; this is why the indie horror scene was doomed. The things that were slithering through the ranks, promoting, slushing, *editing.* They weren't human. Only the old guard like Tim and a few others retained any humanity, only they could stand against the things like Max Booth, Dawn, or fucking Baltisberger.

Tim whirled, pulling the gun out of its holster, and brandished it, seeking the source of John's terrible echoing laughter. He may be inhuman, but one between the eyes would end him, put a stop to the madness Tim himself had helped birth.

"You're gonna fucking die, Baltisberger, you and all your fucking cronies. You're a fucking joke!" He took a step forward, but something snagged his leg, tripping him. Tim sprawled onto the bloody concrete floor. He looked back and watched in horror as the corpse of John Wayne

Comunale pulled itself up his legs, bloody sockets still oozing blood and gray matter. His lips twitched and moved as he made his way toward Tim's face.

"I don't seem to be very funny, Tim, and we never die," Baltisberger said as John Wayne reached blindly and began tearing at Tim's throat with his shattered teeth.

The smoke coalesced into the form of a man, who stared down as Tim was eaten alive. "Long live indie lit, Tim," John said, picking the lit cigar off the ground and taking a short puff. "And long live horror."

* * *

No Pets Allowed

By: Paul Lubaczewski

I have decided that I no longer believe any action-hero stuff I read or watch. I know, you could make a strong case that I never should have, I feel you, but hey, don't we all sort of believe in that crap? Like deep down, don't we all want the Rock to really kick ass like that, we all want the car to be able to handle those corners? What changed my worldview specifically? See, there's always the next day, and on the next day, the hero always looks the same way in every film. He or she looks a bit tired with a taped-up shoulder or ribs, which if it's a particularly well-made film, he will remember to wince about and hold with a soft "I was in an action sequence, but I'm a tough guy" grimace. But that will be the extent of the lasting ill effects. Maybe a limp or something if he has to walk off into the sunset ruggedly. Other than moving slow, and theatrical wincing, not a damned thing wrong with him or her, as long as they remember the wincing and moving slowly, just a normal day in action film-ville.

What about taking a shit? I mean, as a for instance, it's not like it's a personal obsession or anything. There's a lot of stuff involved in the act other than the obvious clenching and unclenching of a few muscles. Where is the realistic next day groaning from the bathroom I ask you? Nobody ever sprains a wrist? Breaks a finger? Try wiping with a sprained wrist or a busted finger, I dare you. How about getting off the toilet with an injured knee? Hell, for that matter reaching back there at all with the obligatory shoulder or rib injury. Take my word for it, after the first post-chaos sit down these are the sort of things that become foremost on your mind. Has it ever gotten a mention? Nope, never. The hero might even "hit the can" but you don't hear one ounce of cursing through the door. Complete horseshit if you ask me.

Also, on a related side note, whoever decided to put child-proof lids on the arthritis strength pain relievers is a sadistic fuck face, and I wish for nothing but the most painful and debilitating injuries to follow him or her all the rest of their days. See how you like pushing down and twisting with carpal tunnel, asshole!

Was there a point to any of those observations? Other than me feeling that somebody needed to speak up and make them? I can hear you yelling it now, your hands tightening on the book or Kindle you're reading these words on. Well of course there is a point, don't be an ass. I may waste time like a champion, but even I wouldn't waste time on that...well unless I was drinking with buddies or something because that'd be a good topic for when you're all a six-pack in.

There's the story of how I got to the point of how I was thinking about the above quite a bit. That rant was all just set up.

One of the things I hate about having an apartment is neighbors. Not all neighbors, some have been fine and I have nothing but nice things to say about them. I guess I more hate the concept of not being able to pick who ends up living next to you and always having to rely on luck of the draw just to know what your home life is going to be like. And if I hate it so much, why do I keep doing it? Trust me, I've been saving for the security deposit on a bigger place outside of town for a while now, maybe rent a house or something. Anything to at least give me some breathing room. Because in an apartment building, you really don't have any no matter how big your place is. You can hear them through the wall, through your door, through your floor, you see them in the hall, they are a part of your life. You may try to avoid contact like the plague, but to some degree, you are living with these people. It's like having a much older sibling or something, you live in the same house you just try to avoid each other and fail.

Like I said though, they aren't all bad. Take Mr. Tyler in 2A, my former next-door neighbor. Guy was a sweetheart. Widower, he'd sold his house and rented this place for himself. Said he didn't like having all that empty space to knock around in all by himself, got sick of taking care of a yard, got sick of hustlers calling him about refinancing or whatever that crap was they sell on TV to swindle old people is. He just liked having a nice little place next to mine (2B) where he and his cat could wile away the hours together without ever having to consider the gutters needing cleaning. Considering the size of the place he'd sold; his rent probably wasn't much more than his property taxes had been. His kids were kind of pissed because they knew every month he lived here was cutting into their inheritance, while the former property was only escalating in value, but he didn't care. And good for him, I say as a man with no children and little chance to ever have any.

He was a nice old duffer, always willing to give advice on maintenance, which was a godsend since waiting on the super could take a lifetime. A guy who was always happy to hang out and tell stories over a beer always had a dad joke handy in greeting. Really, when I first moved into the place, Mr. Tyler was a blessing from heaven, a kind face in the maelstrom of moving into a new apartment and a new neighborhood. Which is where I like to think he went, heaven I mean, not a new neighborhood, though if you think about it... He was a man willing to do a lot of things for a lot of people, except, of course, keeping his nitro pills handier. At least he didn't rot in his apartment for weeks like a lot of old people do when their tickers cease in their appointed task. I had stopped by that day to see if I could borrow a drill so I could put up shelves, twenty minutes later the super showed up with a key. An hour after that a stretcher with a black body bag on it was leaving. Never did find out who got his cat. It was a nice cat.

His shuffling off this mortal coil meant, a couple of weeks later I got to watch the new guy move in. I was trying not to hate him on sight for not being Mr. Tyler. It was hard, you know? Mr. Tyler was like the father I never had, because unfortunately I had been stuck with my dad instead. I kept watching out my window and out the eyehole of my door as the new guy hauled his stuff up from his rental van outside. He looked normal enough, young, which could be problematic, big beard, well built. He looked like just some dude. A dude I hoped wasn't too much of a partier, but you can never tell. Big beards weren't for bikers anymore.

I knew I had to get introductions over with sooner rather than later unless I wanted to hide in my apartment until one of us moved out. So, I waited until I was sure there was nothing else heavy that had to come out of the van and went out into the hallway. He came up the stairs hauling a rather large, and heavy box that clinked and rattled. Seeing me, he set the box down with a clank.

"Umm hi!" I began tentatively. I'm not much of a people person, so this forthrightness was pushing it for me. "I guess you're my new neighbor. I'm Andrew, I'm in 2B."

"Oh, hey! Nice to meet you, I'm Caleb. Let me get this box in, and you can come on in for a beer to say hello properly," he beamed.

"Well, I'm free for a little while, I guess," I replied quickly, mainly because he was serving my favorite brand of beer, free.

"Cool, just follow me in and I'll take the box. Last one thank God," he said.

"If I had known I'd have given you a hand," I lied outrageously.

"Oh, no problem, it was like a free workout," he said as he hefted the clanking box.

Inside his place, it was mainly decorated in Ye Olde Cardboarde Browne. Boxes were stacked more or less everywhere, with the exception of his TV and an elderly-looking couch. Caleb had solid bachelor priorities, the TV was top-notch and already hooked up and ready to go.

"Take a load off on the couch, I'll put this away and be right back with that beer," Caleb said as he made for the hallway off the living room. He wouldn't be gone long, these were not luxurious apartments, there was only so far, he could go without using a sledgehammer. All that was back there was a bedroom a much smaller room that could be a children's room if you had one, and a bathroom, I called them, "beginning and end habitats." You got one of these places at the start of your adult life because they were cheap, and at the end for the exact same reason.

As promised, in no time at all he was back and rustling around the refrigerator in the semi-attached kitchen.

"Man, it's weird to be in here," I mused as Caleb clinked beers around in the fridge.

"How so? The old tenant anti-social?"

My head snapped up in time to see him returning with two bottles. I accepted one and said, "No, the complete opposite. Mr. Tyler who used to live here was the nicest old guy. He used to have me over all the time, guess for someone to talk to. It's weird for it not to be still his place, ya know?"

"So, what happened to him?" Caleb asked as he dug out an easy chair that had been buried in boxes.

"What happens to us all eventually," I replied.

"Oh, well that's a shame," he said with some sincerity.

"Yeah," I nodded, "gonna' miss the old guy."

Caleb held out his bottle, "To old friends and hopefully new ones."

I clinked my bottle and took a swig, hard to leave a guy hanging on something like that.

"So, what brings you here to the great big city," I asked by way of a conversation starter.

"Needed to get away from home for a while, this was all I could really afford."

"But you have a job, right? I mean what are you?"

"I'm a werewolf, but I also have a job," Caleb replied with an absolutely straight face.

Now, you may be reading this and thinking that I would make a big joke about it and we'd laugh and laugh. Or I would get the fuck out of there then and there. If those were your thoughts, you are not a city dweller. A city dweller knows that you never directly confront a crazy person with reality when they say something crazy. They are used to being confronted on their crazy and have set reactions, some of which can often get violently defensive. I was in his place, I did not want a confrontation, I didn't know where any weapons were. What I wanted was a way to change the subject and then get the fuck out of there without him noticing I thought he was ready for the funny farm.

"Well, everybody needs a hobby," I said carefully.

"Don't get me wrong, I'm careful about it. That's what was in that last box, chains for the full moon. I even keep a cane with a silver head and a gun with silver bullets in the apartment, just in case. I'm really fastidious about it."

I nodded slowly as if I was afraid my head would fall off, "Fastidious, nice college word there."

Caleb was quiet for just a moment before his face brightened, "Hey that reminds me, you wouldn't happen to have a stud finder, do you?"

I know I should have already made an excuse to leave without getting more sucked into this crazy town crap, but I didn't. See, I'm not a particularly handy guy, but when I put in my TV Mr. Tyler helped me with just that task and given this sudden opportunity I wanted to show off my masculine studly (ha ha) handiness around the house. Pathetic, huh?

"Don't need one, the guy who lived here before you was a whiz at this stuff and showed me a trick," I replied with a great big stupid grin.

"Really? That is so cool!" Caleb replied with genuine enthusiasm. "Could you do the trick for me?"

Again, I could have begged off, this time I even had enough brain power to consider it. I am not a total idiot. That brainpower fell again before my own deep-seated views on my masculinity. In my defense, I was a bookworm in Junior High School, and I can describe in detail what the inside of a locker looks like with the door closed. I mean since then I growth spurted my way out of constant abuse and even got a gym membership, but some wounds never heal.

"Sure!" I said brightly.

"Cool! Follow me, I need to know roughly where two studs are. I mean in the wall, not us," he laughed.

"Ummm, yeah, sure, let's do it." Was werewolf some kind of a term for a certain type of gay guy, like bear? Even if I wasn't sure, I was already making plans for letting him down easy.

The only decoration in the room in the very back was the box Caleb had brought in earlier. "Basically, I need two bolts set in the far wall, about four feet across."

"Ummm, OK, cool," I said and hurried across the room so I could get this over with. I moved over to the wall and started slapping it the way old Mr. Tyler had shown me, with my head near the wall to catch the correct sound.

After a few minutes of looking stupid I finally confidently turned and pointed to two spots. "There and there should just about do it!"

"Hey, great, that'll save me a ton of time!"

"Glad I could help, hey look, I gotta' get going, I have some stuff I have to work on at my place," I said.

"You sure? I've got plenty of brews."

"Yeah, I've been over here longer than I intended already, maybe another time hey? I mean, you know where to find me," I said as I already began my way down the hall.

Caleb looked a little crestfallen, but bucked up, "Yeah that's true. Anyway, nice to meet you, neighbor."

"Nice to meet you too!" I said with far more enthusiasm than I felt.

And that was that more or less, that was my new neighbor. I mean I'd see Caleb around here or there, but we fell into being just neighbors and nothing more. He was infallibly courteous and friendly when I saw him and I reciprocated as much as I was physically able. I'm not a hugger. Within a couple of weeks of meeting him, I just wrote off the whole werewolf thing as some kind of fad or slang that I didn't know about because it is my firm belief that all of Western civilization will give you stomach cancer if you pay too much attention to it.

A few weeks after he had moved in, Caleb and I were both coming in at the same time. So, there we were, stuck in the building's creaking dilapidated elevator. Frankly, the thing scared the crap out of me, but not quite as much as the concept of using the stairs did because I am an American city dweller and therefore, I distrust all exercise I don't pay a membership to partake in. What can I say, I have a lazy streak in me, call it a byproduct of spending my teen years playing games on Steam and not outdoor ones that involved any degree of sunshine and possible physical distress of any kind.

"How are you doing today?" Caleb opened right up cheerfully. He did everything cheerfully, but he did it like a golden retriever puppy, you couldn't get mad at him.

"All right I guess, another day, 'nuther fifty cents after taxes," I replied.

"I hear ya'," he replied chuckling at my lame assed joke, despite it not deserving it.

There was one of those uncomfortable silences where everyone has run out of small talk and they're waiting for the elevator to JUST HURRY THE FUCK UP ALREADY.

Then Caleb turned to me and said, "Hey, want to come over for a beer or two? I got a mix case at a distributor and hey, share the wealth I always say."

I usually would have passed, but the lure of free beer at that kind of quantity was too strong when combined with my totally absent social life, "Yeah, let me put my groceries away and get a quick shower."

"Hey, great, see you in a bit!" Caleb smiled widely as the elevator finally clanged to a halt.

"Yeah....uhhh....see you soon," I said to his retreating back as soon as I realized what I'd agreed to. This was actual human interaction! Dear God, next thing I'd be joining a book club or something.

So yeah, with a moment to think about it I didn't really want to go over, but what could I do? The free booze hound in me had committed me to this, and now I had to do as he asked or appear rude. I had no way of knowing how long I was going to be living next to Caleb and this was still early enough in our relationship where I could create the kind of sour taste in his mouth that would ensure complaints to the super and calls to the cops for the entire rest of my existence in the building if I wasn't careful.

So, there I was an hour later, knocking on his door. As he opened up, (and it was fast, he must have heard me in the hall) he was already thrusting a beer in my hand. "Come on in, pull up a chair," he said with that ever-present smile of his.

As I followed him in, I took a glance at the bottle in my hand. Local microbrewery, this was good stuff, and usually out of my price range.

Maybe the night would be better than I thought. After I was done perusing the beer for quality, I closed the door and looked around.

I hadn't actually come all the way inside the place since I helped him with his stud finding. (Why hasn't Studfinder become a name for a hookup site? Maybe it has, you should look and report back) It was decorated in a style called Single Guy Loser. I recognized the style immediately since my own apartment showed me to be an aficionado. There was one framed poster for the movie Terminator, a shelf with various action figures in the original packaging, a couch that looked to have seen better days, a very beaten coffee table, one Xbox, and the nicest piece of furniture he owned, an entertainment center on top of which poised the focal point of the whole room, the TV. I relaxed considerably; he was of my tribe.

The TV was on, but the sound of whatever he was streaming had the volume down so we could talk. I did the natural thing in a stranger's home where I wasn't sure I wanted to be; I went to look at the action figures. Most of them were comic book related, which I approved of. There were also a couple of horror movie monster-type ones, which I didn't get judgy about even if they weren't my thing. I couldn't help but notice that most of the boxes were just as pristine as the figures inside. Considering his recent move, Caleb had to be a whizz at packing to keep the boxes from getting scuffed in the shift to the new apartment.

"You into action figures?" Caleb asked as he spotted my interest.

"Used to be, seems like living in the city, money goes faster than it comes in. I've had to curtail collecting and just count myself lucky I haven't had to sell any to make ends meet."

"I hear you; I can see the city making it tight, and I haven't even been here long enough for bills to start coming in yet. Everything costs more here."

"That is the joy of buying stuff online, at least you can cut some of the markup that way," I replied.

He smiled, as always, with total sincerity, "Man, you are just full of good advice. Hey, you play X-box at all?"

"I am a single male in my twenties, the only way that answer would have been no is if I preferred online gaming, but the Xbox also lets me watch movies in 4K."

"Exactly! Hey, you play 'Eye Gouger 3, The Wrath of the Marbles' yet?"

I felt extremely embarrassed to say what I said next, it was an admission of failure on many levels, "I haven't been able to find a copy for less than a hundred bucks yet."

"You wanna' play? Cause I got it!" Caleb grinned knowingly.

And that was pretty much so a bunch of hours gone right there. Come on, in this game, you had to kill various baddies and then gouge various marbles out of the heads of your fallen victims until you found special marbles that opened secret passages or solved puzzles. The final boss was a giant eyeball that shot acid eye slime at you. Who in the hell didn't want to do that for hours? It took me 45 minutes just to find the one Aggie I needed. The cat's eye probably took looking up a walkthrough.

It was getting pretty late, and to be honest, my hand was starting to cramp. For that matter, with all the beer we'd drunk my brain was starting to cramp as well. "Take my controller man, I gotta' hit the can."

Caleb took it from me and smoothly transitioned into the game. He gave a quick glance out of the corner of his eye, "You know where it is, right?"

"Dude, you got like one hallway. Worse to worse I'll find it by process of elimination," I replied, getting to my feet with only a minor wobble.

"Speaking of which, just don't do any eliminations until you're sure what room you're in, ok?"

"And dishonor the good neighbor code? Nay sir! I will not release until I am sure I am aiming for porcelain. Now don't get killed before I get back OK?" I said as I made my way toward the dark hall.

"Got it."

I am ashamed to say, I did not open the right door first try out. When I flicked on the lights, I thought I recognized the room he wanted me to find a stud in. The only decorations in the place were four heavy, very metal shackles bolted to the wall. Well, that explained the clanking when he was bringing that last box in. Deciding that Caleb didn't seem quiet enough and didn't keep to himself enough to be a serial killer, I figured it wasn't my place to judge anyone's sex life. And really, with the serial killer thing, listen to any damned neighbor or co-worker interview after the bodies are found. It's always, "He was so quiet," they almost never say "Gregarious to the point of being annoying sometimes."

On try two, I did indeed find blessed porcelain and was able to release the pressure which had by that point started to make my teeth float. The bathroom, judging from the three or four square inches that were directly in front of me as I exhaled with relief, seemed normal enough at least.

It was time to buck up, and completely pretend that I hadn't seen the shackles. I could do this, all I had to say was nothing at all.

"Dude, what kind of sex games do you get up to?" flopped right out of my mouth the second I walked into the room because drunk brain was not on speaking terms with sober brain at the moment.

Caleb didn't freak, instead, he laughed and said, "Told you, man, I'm a werewolf."

For some reason, this seemed completely logical to me at that moment. Some reason being a lot of beers of course. "Yeah, right, you said."

I looked at the controller for the game and realized how cooked I was. "I think I gotta' head home. Not cause of the werewolf thing, right, I'm not like a sex shamer or prejudiced or anything. It's because even though it's......I don't know how many steps it is, but I know it ain't many, anyway, if I stay much longer I will not make it that far."

Caleb nodded, he'd been going beer for beer with me, he understood my predicament. "Say, before you go, I wanted to give you something."

"A beer or two for the road?"

"No, but like, you can grab a couple if you want," he replied. While he laboriously got to his feet to get something, I weaved my way over to the case and deftly snagged three beers with one hand, putting the necks between my fingers.

When I turned back toward my exit, Caleb was standing there holding a cane. "Here, I want you to have this. You're my first friend in the city, and I'd feel terrible if something happened."

"Like one day I couldn't walk without a limp and would need a cane or something?" I asked with a blank expression.

He looked at the cane for a second and blinked. "Huh! Yeah, I guess you could use it for that too. No, the head of the cane. It's solid silver dude."

"In case I can't make rent?"

He blinked at me this time, "No, dude, it's heavy. If you needed to, you could bash someone's head in with it."

"Does it matter if it's silver? I mean, what is that? A wolf's head? The size of that thing could bash in most people's heads even if it was steel."

Caleb grinned at that, "Yeah, most PEOPLE'S."

"Why did you stress that last word?"

"It's why I keep a loaded .38 by the door with silver bullets in it. In case someone needs to come in here. It keeps it fair. But seriously, you're my friend. I want you to have this, please. I'm begging, here, take it," he said thrusting the cane out to me.

I mean, what do you do in this situation? A drunk friend makes you a spectacular gift? I had enough drinking experience to know that the only way to defuse this was to accept, and then give it back when Caleb sobered up tomorrow.

"Sure, thanks!" I said with the small amount of enthusiasm I could manage.

"Thank you so much!" he practically gasped when I took the cane.

"No, you're the one giving something away, so I say the thank yous here. I'm pretty sure that's how that works traditionally. Speaking of away, I gotta go there while I still have legs to carry me," I said.

I couldn't help but notice that he hadn't lied, there was a gun on a small bookshelf next to the door. I didn't have a lot of experience with guns, so that was the kind of thing that would automatically catch my eye now that I was looking in exactly the right direction.

The next day was a nothing day. I was rough from the night before, so my sole contribution to the world was in terms of the economy. i.e. I went to the local deli and bought some junk food and a couple of six-packs of beer. I spent my day watching TV, eating what could only be called sugar and salt in puffed and bar forms, and slowly sipped on a beer hoping to feel good enough at some point to go to sleep and try again tomorrow.

That was exactly what I was still working on when the sun went down and the moon came up.

The entertainment was classic horror, by which I mean 80's Italian zombie-related schlock. I was just beginning to drowse slightly in my lazy boy when I heard the muffled growl from next door. I figured, if Caleb had felt anything like I had this morning, he'd probably followed my example and had fallen asleep on top of the volume button of his remote.

Then I heard a roar, followed by a metallic crashing noise.

Naw.....it couldn't be...

Despite myself telling me it was nothing, I clambered to my feet and made for the door to see what in the hell the ruckus was all about. As an afterthought, I grabbed the cane that I had left by the door when I came in last night. In case it was something more serious than late-night movies on max volume, the cane constituted the entirety of my home defense arsenal. In life I have always been more of a fan of thick doors, massive locks, and if they failed, giving the nice robbers anything they wanted since they were obviously very strong. I know how shitty my stuff was, I damned well wasn't getting killed for it.

Considering I didn't want to be killed over my own belongings, it kind of makes me wonder what in the fuck I was thinking stepping outside my door to check on a noise like that.

I got out into the hallway just in time for my other neighbor, Mrs. Hansey, to open her door.

"What's all that racket?" she demanded.

"I have no idea, ma'am," I said to the elderly African-American woman. "I just came out to check myself."

I heard another growl, and this time there was no mistaking it. It was definitely coming from inside Caleb's place. This was the moment you find out what you're made of. When you rise to the occasion. You put the biscuit in the basket. The cream rises to the top. It was at a moment like that you proved to the whole world just who in the hell they were dealing with here.

I stood stock still in the hallway gaping at Caleb's door, because what I was made of at the time, and whom the world was dealing with, was a lightly buzzed weenbag. At least until the door flew off the hinges. Immediately after that, I did not stride into the fray, I more flinched in a dramatic yet embarrassingly full-blown wimp fashion. Standing there in the doorway was an important confirmation of an eternal question. Did werewolves turn into full wolves or more of that thing from the Howling and Dog Soldiers? The answer definitely leaned toward the Howling, right down to the big ears. The only difference was this thing was only 6'10" max and not 8 feet like they looked in the movies. Hollywood never gets anything right, I swear.

"Lord have mercy!" Mrs. Hansey breathed.

"Ma'am, I would sincerely suggest you go back inside, I'll try to hold him off," someone more heroic than me said using my voice. Mrs. Hansey proved to be a sensible woman, she didn't say a word to try and talk me out of it, but a second later I heard her throwing bolts on the door.

Which left me with a conundrum. I had flinched my way out into the middle of the hallway. What I could only assume was Caleb, unless he didn't tell the super about a REALLY exotic pet he was keeping, was at this point between me and everything. The stairs were just past his apartment, he was closer to my door than I was at this point and some complete dumb ass had said something about keeping the beast away from Mrs. Hansey's door which was locked up tight taking up the final direction. Not that I wanted to go that way since it dead-ended shortly after her door, which would only delay things as far as my painful demise.

I looked at the cane in my hand. Caleb had given it to me for a reason, he knew I might need to protect myself. That meant I wasn't completely screwed, only mostly screwed, which is completely screwed with unreasonable hope. The creature lunged toward me with drooly teeth, and red angry eyes, and claws, and all kinds of unpleasant crap. I did the only thing I could think to do; I hit him with the cane. Nobody, and I mean nobody, was more shocked than me when the thing yelped and flinched back away from me.

I started circling toward the stairs swinging wildly with the cane, Mrs. Hansey was locked up tight, the thing had come from Caleb's apartment, and I still didn't have a clear path to mine. Right now I needed to get away or club the thing into submission. There was a convergence there, for me to get to the stairs I'd need the thing to back up a bit, and that meant it was clubbing baby harp seals time.

I wound up and hit the thing in its shoulder with everything I had. I had aimed for the head, but in my defense, I'm not a big martial combat guy, so me even hitting it counted as a victory. It yelped again and drew back a little further giving me room. Holy crap! This was actually working! Sorry for Caleb, but he had to have known it might come to this, he gave me the cane. I wound up and swung for its head again, hoping to end this without having to run for the stairs. Damned shame it got the wooden shaft in its suddenly upthrust claw. This had not happened to Claude Rains in the old black-and-white flick. Lon Chaney Jr. had certainly not proceeded to bite his cane in half and throw the halves indifferently over his shoulder. In direct contrast to film fiction that was exactly what Caleb did.

And then those claws lashed out catching me on the chest, hurting like hell for just a moment before I was distracted by the blow sending me airborne. The good news here was, I made it to the steps. The bad news was I did not proceed to use them in their designed manner, preferring instead to painfully roll down toward the lobby. Bouncing off the walls and then the rails and then the steps in an exceedingly painful, yet comical manner.

I lay in a heap at the first-floor landing wondering if I was going to bleed to death first or was Caleb going to have to come down and finish me off for a more merciful end. I pulled myself up enough to lean back against the stairwell and looked up, waiting for death to descend on me. I took a quick look at my front and decided that Caleb was going to need another swipe to kill me, the bleeding seemed to be slowing down considerably already. I hadn't broken anything either, so that was a blessing, Caleb would have to do that all by himself when he got there. Maybe it would keep him busy for the rest of the night and save others this bloody end.

So, what I'm saying is I was pretty resigned to my fate. I thought that I could get back up, but I hurt all over, so I wasn't going to set any land speed records for running away. I also was without a weapon, since both the cane and the gun Caleb had mentioned had a werewolf between me and them. I was lying there waiting for my life to pass before my eyes when I learned something amazingly interesting.

Werewolves have a devil of a time with stairs.

Because their rear paw is supporting so much weight, they end up slightly overbalanced. Their animal brain knows this and is rightly uncomfortable about the whole thing. So while I waited, Caleb came into view. He took one step down, put his paw in place, tested it carefully, and then daintily put the other paw on the same step. There was a long pause, and a worried expression on the monster's face before it was willing to try another step.

I decided that maybe I was going to live after all. I dragged myself to my feet and bolted for the front door. Well, more staggered in an aggressive manner. As my hand fell on the handle I paused. Yeah, I might get out, but Mrs. Hansey was a nice old broad. Sure, she'd bolted her door, but Caleb probably had too, and look how long that slowed the monster down. I stood there listening to the thing's claws slowly clacking their way down the steps.

The building did have an elevator. It opened on the other side of Caleb's door.

Caleb did have a gun.

I was way too cowardly to be a hero.

So, imagine my surprise when I found myself standing there waiting for the elevator. I hoped to God the damned thing wasn't broken again, especially since I was beginning to be able to see the werewolf's shadow as he worked down steps.

I could not believe I was doing this stupid shit.

I also couldn't believe that Mr. Nusbaum. from 3C was somehow already in there when the doors finally did open.

"Afternoon," he said as he began to get out.

"It's night. Are we not looking out the window again Mr. Nusbaun?"

"I don't like to be nosy," he shrugged.

Caleb chose that moment to howl.

"But I won't mind riding back up with you," he said. "I didn't need the damned milk anyway, and if Miriam doesn't like it, she can come down here and deal with whatever the hell that was herself."

We didn't talk after the door closed. The only thing to discuss was the monster, and neither of us really wanted to acknowledge it to the other. When the door opened on the second floor I took a quick look out to make sure the coast was clear.

"Well, are you getting out?" demanded Mr. Nusbaum impatiently.

Instead of responding, I ran for Caleb's as quietly and quickly as I could. Mrs. Hansey's was quiet as a tomb, but since I hadn't heard anything, I figured the door was still intact. I couldn't help but wonder if she had called the cops yet. I kind of hoped she hadn't. If this didn't work I had no idea what some cops were going to do about it. You hate to see people get hurt by accident like that. Come to think of it, I'd hate to see me get hurt anymore on purpose, but at least I knew what to expect at this point.

I couldn't see Caleb as I crept the last distance toward his apartment, but I could still hear the clacks of his claws on the stairs. Once inside his apartment....wow it was a mess. He'd blown through like a tornado on his way to get out the door. The shelf that had the gun on it was knocked over and I couldn't see the thing anywhere. This was not convenient. I pulled the shelf up just to see a scatter of books, but no guns.

Sighing, which was a surprise considering how keyed up I was, I began to dig through the pile of literature. Just as I was picking up a particularly heavy volume to set it aside, I heard a loud clunk on the floor. Shoving aside the rest of the books and magazines, there it was, the gun Caleb had specifically let me know about! It occurred to me he might have been bluffing about the silver bullets to put me at ease. I mean, how did you even get silver bullets made if you aren't Gary Busey trying to impress his niece and nephew?

Misgivings aside, I picked up the gun. I had to admit it felt more reassuring in the face of the monstrosity I had faced than the cane had. I just needed to man up and go and face my fears. My fears, in this case, being a huge werewolf with giant fangs and claws. So, you have to admit, more intense than a fear of heights.

Fangs that chose just that moment to clamp down on my shoulder.

Bastard could move pretty quietly when he wanted to, no mistake about that.

I did the only thing I could do, I screamed bloody murder from the pain, probably ensuring Mrs. Hansey would never leave her apartment again as long as she lived. Caleb made to shake me like a rag doll. The good news was, he had more shirt than shoulder clenched in his teeth. The bad news was, that he did have some shoulder and flesh tore just as easily as the shirt did from those fangs, and I went flying across the room to slam into the far wall. Probably directly on a stud by the feel of it.

It took me a moment for my eyes to refocus. Unfortunately, what they ended up focusing on was Caleb, and he was coming right at me with evil intent in his bloodshot wolfie eyes. Some little voice that represented my feeble survival instinct screamed to make itself heard over my internal panic. My scientific and logical self wasn't coming up with anything, so it allowed survival instinct to have the floor. It informed all of the voices in my head of something incredibly important to remember in this situation. I didn't drop the gun when Caleb had flung me against the wall.

Nothing left to do but find out if Caleb went to the same gunsmith that Gary Busey did and fire away!

I emptied the chamber, and when the smoke cleared, Caleb was no longer coming after me. Instead, he was on the floor beginning to look increasingly human, but with more bullet holes in him than were the usual for a healthy person.

As tired and as injured as I was, I knew one thing, and one thing only.

I was going to have to talk to Mrs. Hansey about getting our stories straight.

Between the fall down the steps and the getting hurled around like a rag doll, I got quite a few boo-boos at that moment. Ones that have not healed as of yet, and therefore make me forever doubt the morning-after scenes in any action movie I will ever watch again. It takes a lot of work to train yourself to wipe left-handed is all I'm saying here.

I am not in trouble with the law, Mrs. Hansey swore up and down to the officers that Caleb had gone plumb loco, and if I hadn't shot him he'd have killed us all. My injuries certainly agreed with that theory. I am not in trouble, but, I have decided to take that money I've been socking away to move out into the country and to do just that instead of just thinking about it. I'll just have to deal with the commute after I find a place.

Because, unlike the concussive injuries, the bite and the claw marks, they healed right up.

Which probably means I'm a werewolf now, so that pretty much so blows.

It's going to take me a little while to get out of my lease and get a new place rented. In the meantime, I've been calling around to hardware stores to get a stud finder.

Slippery Shit

By: John Wayne Comunale

Jacob knew he was running through the woods naked but couldn't remember why. It was dark, and low-hanging branches cut into his shins and smacked his genitals, but something inside would not let him stop. Despite his physical pain and confusion, an urge spurred Jacob on pushing him to keep going.

Was he being chased? Was he fleeing the scene of a crime? Did he commit a crime? Was *he* a criminal? Question after question raced through his head with no answers, yet he continued running despite pinecones and rocks slicing through the pads of his feet with each step.

He ducked narrowly missing a branch when a sudden sensation in his gut triggered the first memory. A hot wet burst of gas provided slight relief and showered the back of his legs in runny moist spatter. Slickness spread steadily down his inner thighs all but eliminating any friction thereby giving him an edge as he continued pumping his legs propelling himself forward.

Something about the viscosity of the warm spray against his skin shook loose a small piece of the puzzle from his otherwise shrouded memory. Jacob remembered a bar, a salad bar. No, not just a salad bar, a whole buffet with warming trays of various meats floating in questionably colored, tepid, mystery liquid.

The buffet was in a dark loud place, and despite the menagerie of food, the only smell he recalled was an overwhelming aroma of coconut. Not real coconut, but the kind produced chemically for suntan lotion like he was on Spring break. There was something wrong going on at this place though. Someone was mad, really mad. Jacob tried to pull more details from his murky memory but there was nothing left to hold onto, and the image slipped from his grasp completely. All he knew for sure was whatever happened at this 'buffet'; whatever went *wrong,* it involved him. He wasn't sure how, but deduced it was most likely the reason he was running.

A cramp twisted his stomach granting escape to another wet fart that sent a second hot helping of brown gush spitting from his asshole shellacking the back of his legs with a second coat of the stuff. Jacob cried out from the burning sensation accompanying his sudden expulsion, but the fire made his memory slightly clearer.

He remembered eating food while watching a show, a live show. There was dancing and the music was loud, overpowering even. Jacob realized it wasn't a show, but a single woman dancing naked. He was at a strip club eating food he'd gotten from the buffet, but if that's all he'd done then why was he running?

He hurdled a log in his path, and a tremendous spray of liquid shit rained down upon it in mid-leap. There was no warning this time, and though his situation was becoming dire he continued to run. A moment later he saw himself at the table again, but the plate in front of him was empty, and something else was different too. His pants were wet and warm.

"My fart!" Jacob called out as he suddenly remembered more.

A fart wrenched itself from Jacob's ass at the exact moment of recollection, and the force of his exclamation ejected more bits of semi-soft gelatinous feces with it. He remembered now. He'd farted in his chair and accidentally shit his pants. That was how this started. The strip club buffet was the cause of his dismay. He was sure of that now only it didn't explain why he found himself presently running naked through the woods at night.

The memories were flowing now but not fast enough to put the whole story together. Jacob's foot came down in something soft and squishy, and he instantly recognized the sensation as having stepped in a pile of shit. He continued to run, but the thought of shit covering his bare foot and filling the spaces between his toes made him sick to his stomach. His asshole released another sticky moist carpet bomb, and he stopped thinking about the shit on his foot.

Now he remembered being in a bathroom stall, a filthy bathroom stall at the strip club. He'd just flushed the toilet and was watching the water in the bowl swirl, but it wasn't shit he was flushing, it was his pants. Why did he flush his pants down the toilet? Jacob answered his own question when his asshole opened up again to jettison another soupy blast of the mealy paste his digestive tract made of the strip club buffet meal.

His lungs burned from sucking wind, and his leg muscles were twisting themselves into one giant cramp, but Jacob refused to stop running. His anxiety spiked when he thought he heard howls coming from behind him, and he pushed himself even harder as more memories flashed across his mind.

He saw water spilling out over the rim of the clogged toilet flooding the entire bathroom. He remembered wiping his ass with his shirt when the stall door burst open, and one of the bouncers yanked him out by his shoulders. There was yelling and shoving, and Jacob accidentally shoved his shit-smeared shirt in the bouncer's face. There was more yelling, some vomiting, more pushing, and even a few punches thrown before he remembered racing through the showroom, past the stage, and toward the exit all while expelling his telltale trail.

Jacob saw the parking lot, watched himself run past his own car, and then dash into the woods behind the club. As far as he could determine he'd eaten bad meat from the strip club buffet, shit his pants, flushed them down the toilet, and wiped his ass with his shirt. Then he flooded the bathroom before sprinting naked into the woods after an altercation with a bouncer.

It was all pretty succinct, but Jacob still didn't know where he was, or why he needed to keep running. His stomach lurched as pressure began to build again in his bowels. Suddenly, he could see a break in the trees ahead and his drive renewed. He burst through the opening and found himself in the middle of the unlit two-lane road that cut through the woods between highways.

He finally stopped, and though it was night, the heat of the day had been soaked up by the asphalt and burned the bottom of his bloody shredded feet. Struggling to catch his breath, he bent with his hands on his knees gasping for air when the pressure in his colon reached a critical point.

Hot watery shit exploded from Jacob's aching asshole, the force of which stretched his opening beyond its limits. The spongy flesh tore like wet construction paper from the intensity, and the pain would've been excruciating if a car hadn't hit him at the same moment.

Jacob didn't see it coming, the car that hit him, but he remembered spinning head over heels in the air as muddy shit spewed from his ruined sphincter like an open fire hydrant. His body made enough rotations to hit himself in the face with the airborne excrement expulsion twice before his head mercifully crumpled against the road, and suddenly shit in the face didn't matter much anymore.

Several feet beyond his broken form a shit-covered car's brakes screeched as it swerved to a stop on the side of the road.

***

He watched them from the woods' edge silent and unseen. Both of them had looked directly at him while scanning the side of the road without realizing he was there. The two men walked in a daze around their vehicle trying to piece together how it came to be covered in a smattering of lumpy wet shit and blood like cinnamon oatmeal with raspberry jam, and only slightly less appealing. The two saps had just saved him a heap of trouble.

He stifled a chuckle as the two of them walked around and around the car looking from it to the wet smear on the pavement twenty-five feet behind it, and back again. All the evidence that they'd hit someone, or something was there except the body, and its absence put them both in a dizzying state of confusion.

He'd been chasing him through the woods from Club Olympus, the naked shitting man, and was in fact nearly upon him when he'd dashed out across the dark road. For once, he was glad to be a few steps behind otherwise he too would've been flung ass over tea kettle by the speeding hatchback making for a most inauspicious ending to his storied career as the Dick-Lick Bandit.

Now that the man was dead the Bandit would never get to make him feel beautiful, but it wasn't a total loss. He'd get some use out of him yet, only not as he'd originally intended but even dead, he'd come in handy. A guy had to eat, right?

"Oh man, oh man, oh man!" The smaller of the two men was beginning to come unraveled, and his voice carried easily on the cool night air from the road. "What are we gonna' do?"

The larger man silently studied the puddle behind the car like he was trying to will it to become a different substance, anything but blood.

"This is shit, man!" The smaller man was yelling and emphatically pointing at the drippy translucent slop running from the hood of the car all the way down the back hatch. "I mean literally, dude! The car is covered in real actual shit! Dude! Dude!"

"Okay, okay I know," the bigger man said. "Just shut up and let me think for a second."

"What the hell is there to think about? We hit a guy who was obviously filled with a lot of shit, and he exploded on impact. Case closed. Let's get the hell out of here!"

"Hold on." The bigger man was much calmer and even-toned than his pint-sized counterpart. "I think maybe we need to call someone."

"Call someone!" The smaller man became more animated now throwing his arms up in the air gesturing emphatically. "Call someone? Like who? The bio-hazard squad? *Unsolved Mysteries*? The good people at Charmin? I know you can't mean the police, because that would be as crazy as an exploding shit-filled man."

"You don't think we need to report . . . something? It's your car dude, I mean don't you need it for like the insurance or something?"

"I'm sorry, was that an actual serious question?" The smaller man had calmed slightly, but the bite wasn't gone from his disposition as he held his hand to the side of his head pantomiming a phone call. "Oh hello. Could you send an adjuster to my house, please? What? Well, we hit a man and he exploded into shit all over the car and while the cosmetic damage is minimal, I'm really worried about the baked-in human waste causing issues down the line."

"I guess it would be a little tricky to explain," the bigger man said walking from the puddle back to the car. "But shouldn't there be something else left of this guy? Like an empty skin suit, or some bones, or like *anything* else from inside the human body besides shit? I could've sworn I saw a body land in the road behind us in the mirror. It's gone now, but something left that puddle back there."

"Who knows dude?" The smaller man was trying to find a way to open the passenger door without his bare hands coming into contact with bloody shit-juice, a task he would find difficult to complete. "Maybe his skin melted, or he ascended into heaven or some shit, I don't know? What I do know is we need to get some water on this shit before it starts to dry. It'll ruin the paint!"

In reality, the twisted body of the naked shitting man lay at the Bandit's feet hidden by underbrush and shadows. He looked down at the caved-in face and shook his head. If there was one place this literal dead sack of shit was going it wasn't heaven. The car's engine started, and the Bandit looked up to see both of the men back in the car now. They sat on the side of the road running the windshield wipers for two full minutes before finally driving away, a broken piece of the plastic bumper noisily scraping the concrete as they went.

The Bandit stayed still until the scraping sound faded completely into the night. Then, he grabbed the nude corpse by the foot, and drug it deeper into the woods.

-end-

I'm No Jeff Strand

By: Bridgett Nelson

Piano music drifted through the restaurant. Candlelight flickered on the white, cloth-covered tables and created a warm, shadowy, *romantic* ambiance. Waiters wearing actual tuxedos stood by, ready and willing to be at our beck and call.

I looked at Tiernan. He looked at me. We smiled over our caramelized banana, banana sorbet, and banana cake. Then he cleared his throat and gave a quick nod to our waiter. I watched as the waiter then signaled to the piano player. The beginning notes of "Sweet Caroline" swept across the room, as the pianist, with great theatricality, played Neil Diamond's signature song.

I had to stifle my giggle. It was our two-year anniversary as boyfriend and girlfriend, so I knew Tiernan was trying to be romantic. My *name* was Caroline, so, of course, the song made sense.

However…

I'd graduated from West Virginia University, which Tiernan knew. What he apparently *didn't* know was that my Mountaineers had an intense rivalry with Pitt—a rivalry known as the 'Backyard Brawl.' The schools were only about eighty miles apart, and when our various teams competed, we Mountaineers had a few snazzy lyrics we liked to add to "Sweet Caroline" when it played over the loudspeakers. They went something like this...

Sweet Caroline...

Eat shit Pitt!

Good times never seemed so good...

Eat shit! Eat shit! Eat shit!

I've been inclined...

Eat shit Pitt!

To believe they never would...

(Admit it, you're totally singing it in your head right now, aren't you?)

Was it tactless and crass? It sure as hell was! But, damn, it felt good to scream those lyrics in the midst of a football or basketball game. Frickin' Pitt...

I knew Tiernan had sweet intentions, but my mind kept venturing back to, well, *shit* throughout the entirety of the song. I'm gonna guess that probably wasn't what he was striving for. After it finished, the pianist immediately began playing *our* song, "Housewares Employee" featured in The Evil Dead musical. That's when it finally dawned on me something was up.

Tiernan reinforced my suspicions when he got down on one knee, pulled a teal-blue box from his jacket pocket, gave me a big smile, and said...

"You're the reason I breathe, Caroline."

sound of a phonograph needle being pulled violently across a vinyl record

What the hell kind of thing was that to say? I was under the impression his heart and lungs were doing that job. But, it was me? Fuck! That was a lot of pressure.

"...and so, having said all these deeply personal things, I was hoping you'd do me the immense honor of being my wife." He slid an enormous princess-cut diamond on my finger.

I had no idea what he'd said. He could have recited the Taco Bell menu for all I knew. But I loved him, and I wanted to be his wife, no matter how badly he was fucking up this proposal.

I nodded my head to accept, and the restaurant erupted into polite, restrained applause.

Tiernan and I hugged. He whispered, "I love you," in my ear. I whispered it back. We both sat down and continued eating our phallic-banana dessert. Inside, something occurred to me, and I was in turmoil. I couldn't believe my life had come to this. When I'd met him, I didn't think we'd stick.

But now, I would be signing all future documents as *Caroline Felicity Diamond.*

Oh, I didn't mention that? Tiernan's surname was Diamond. Yeah, my life had come full circle and was maybe just a little bit...stupid.

***

Tiernan was a big guy. Although his name often led people to believe he was Irish, he wasn't. He was born in North Dakota to Swedish immigrants, and that's exactly how he looked. Tall, lanky, blonde, blue-eyed, with very thin lips. He was...not my type. Yet, I fell in love with him anyway.

We just had so much in common— desserts, horror movies....

Okay, maybe we didn't have that much in common, but he made me laugh, and that was important in a relationship. *Or maybe he said stupid shit, and I silently made fun of him.*

Either way, I was glad we were engaged. I couldn't wait to see what our kids looked like. Would they be tall and fair like their dad, or short and swarthy like their mom? My family hailed from Spain and parts of Portugal. I had curly brown hair, hazel eyes, olive skin...and I was curvy. Not overweight, just curvy. Even though she wasn't Spanish, I always said if you pictured Salma Hayek post-baby, that was an accurate comparison.

"What should we watch?" Tiernan asked.

"Something scary!"

"Obviously."

"Not one of those artsy-fartsy films that are supposed to be scary but are really just grainy footage of nothing."

"I liked that movie, Car."

"I know you did, Tier. Bless your heart."

After we'd settled on a newer release we'd both heard was good, I gave him a lingering look.

"Babe, can I ask you a question?"

"Sure."

"What did you mean by the 'you're the reason I breathe' line when you proposed?"

"That I couldn't live without you. That I'd die if we couldn't be together."

"Kind of an overblown statement, don't you think? And loaded. What the hell am I supposed to do with that?" I threw myself back on the couch, the back of my hand strewn across my forehead. "Oh, the pressure!"

"It was meant to be romantic."

"Okay. I get it." I sat up and kissed the tip of his nose. We watched the movie holding hands.

Afterward, we got it on, and it was *good.*

Huh. Maybe that's why I loved him.

***

I worked as a registered nurse at the medical center in our town, which meant long hours and a lot of stress. Once a week, my co-workers would plan a night of drinking, karaoke, and other forms of debauchery. I couldn't decide if I wanted to go that night, so I called Tier to get his opinion.

His office phone rang and rang. I tried his cell, but it went immediately to voice mail, so I tried the office number one last time. It was picked up. "This is Jon, how can I help you?"

Jon was Tiernan's best friend. "Hey, Jon, I need to talk to Tiernan for a sec. Can you put him on?"

There was a brief hesitation. "He's not here, Car. I'll leave him a note to let him know you called."

"That's fine. Any idea where he is?"

Another slight pause. "No clue."

"Okay, no problem. Just tell him to call me when he has a chance."

"Will do!"

We said our goodbyes and hung up. I got back to work. Later that night at the karaoke bar, I killed it singing "Ice Ice Baby."

***

The engagement party my mom threw for us was...interesting.

"Do you know any of these people?" Tiernan asked.

"Nope," I admitted. I was not close to my family. "Just smile and look happy."

A woman with a patch over her left eye was staring at me from the bulging right one. "Caroline, it's your Aunt Ginger! You remember me, right?"

"Oh, Aunt Ginger!" I gave her a hug, careful to avoid her face. "Of course, I remember you."

"I knew you would. I told Carl I was unforgettable after that present I got you for your 12th birthday." She looked at me expectantly.

"You're, uh, unforgettable all right!"

She gave a croaking laugh and kissed my cheek, her froggy eye insanely close. I let out a yelp.

"What's wrong, dear?"

Groping my leg, I yelled, "Cramp!" I jumped around a little, trying to look miserable. "Tiernan here is going to help me walk it off, but so nice seeing you!" I grabbed his hand, and off we went.

"Caroline, Tiernan...nice to see you both!"

An elderly bald man—no, I take that back...he had one strip of shiny, dyed black hair combed across his scalp; *one*—walked toward us, his arms outstretched. He noticed our confused expressions. "Caroline, it's your papa, Dirk. You know, like the porn star, Dirk Diggler from *Boogie Nights*?" He flexed his flabby body.

"Gramps?" I gulped.

"Yes! Impressive, right?" He did a box squat.

"Wow," Tiernan said. "We were just on our way to the punch bowl, but we'll be sure to talk to you a little later."

Papa Dirk Diggler smiled and ventured off into the crowd. Speechless, we headed to the refreshments table, just as several members of Tiernan's family broke into a spontaneous flashmob. They were dancing their hearts out in a very lascivious manner to The Macarena.

As we stared in fascinated horror at the spectacle, a younger guy wandered over. He smiled. Both of his front teeth were missing. "I'm not sure we've met, Caroline, but I'm your cousin, Anakin."

"Ana...kin?"

"You have a cousin named Anakin, love?" Tiernan asked, with not a small amount of fear in his voice.

"I, uh, guess I do! It's nice to meet you, cousin Anakin." I shook his sweaty hand and then walked with purpose to a dark corner, where, hopefully, our mutant families couldn't find me. My fiancé followed.

"So, I was thinking..." Tiernan began.

"That we shouldn't have children?" I finished.

"Bingo."

***

A couple of weeks after our eye-opening engagement party, the freak-outs, and full-body shuddering still hadn't eased. Neither of us was close with our family, yet since the last reunion I'd attended, it seemed the DNA in our bloodlines had gone from '*almost* normal' to 'what the fuck was that?'

"Maybe we should elope," Tiernan suggested.

"I'm down with that." I wandered into the kitchen.

"Where are you going?" Tiernan asked.

"I'm making some popcorn for our movie night."

"Don't bother, babe. I think I'm going to head home. I've got a rager of a headache, and I just want to sleep."

"Oh." I was surprised by the weight of my disappointment. I'd been looking forward to some snuggle time with my guy. Pushing aside my selfish thoughts, I gave him a hug. "I'm sorry you're feeling shitty, Tier. Go home and get some rest."

"Thanks, doll. I'll see you tomorrow." We kissed, and he left.

I sat around my apartment for a while, antsy and out of sorts. Maybe I should stop by the corner deli we both liked and get Tiernan some chicken noodle soup. I mean, facts are facts—

chicken noodle soup made everything better. Hell, maybe I'd even deliver it wearing nothing but my trench coat and some sparkly pink nipple tassels! Knowing how much Tiernan would love that, I hurried to the bathroom to hop in the shower.

An hour later, I was regretting my decision. It was cold. Like, sub-Arctic cold, and my trench coat was rather drafty. One positive...the cold was keeping my tassels nice and perky. The line at the deli was long (who the hell wanted deli food at ten o'clock on a Thursday night?), and when I finally got to the front, all the soups were sold out. Except for one.

"Uh, I guess I'll have a large Duck's Blood soup, please."

"Oh, splendid! You're the first customer brave enough to try it. It's delicious. I use the blood from my very own ducks, and dry my own fruits...."

Her voice faded, and I felt faint. What the fuck was I buying? I figured the red coloring was just dye or beets or something.

"Here you go." She handed me a plastic container filled with the bloody, fruity concoction. I took it reluctantly. "That'll be $48.96."

"I'm sorry. Say again?"

"$48.96."

"I think there must be a mistake. I only got the soup."

"Right. I charge by the ounce for such a rare delicacy. Will that be cash or charge?"

***

I walked down the street carrying the murdered duck juice, my lady bits no doubt covered by icy shards. In my head, I could hear the final desperate "quack" as that crazy bitch sliced Mr. Ducky's neck and drained his life's blood for her grody soup. I'd tell Tier it was savory strawberry or something. No way we were wasting fifty-dollar soup.

When I finally arrived at his condo, I seriously believed one quick swipe of Tiernan's tongue while eating my pussy might shatter the lips like the robot frozen in liquid nitrogen in *Terminator 2*. That was a cheery thought.

When I reached his door on the fourth floor, I quietly let myself in. I couldn't wait to give my guy some TLC. I was a nurse, after all…it's what I did.

First, I'd make him take some ibuprofen, and we'd shower together. Then I'd give him a massage to loosen up those tense muscles he always had around his neck and shoulders. Next, I'd ride him like the nasty cowgirl I was, followed immediately by some delicious duck blood so he'd have a nice, full belly when we fell asleep in each other's arms.

I knew how to take care of my man.

A long, drawn-out moan came from Tier's bedroom. *Poor guy, he must be feeling really shitty.* I unbuttoned my coat so that it hung open, exposing my nipple tassels, grabbed the soup container (which, now that it wasn't heated, appeared to be clotting), and opened the bedroom door with a flourish…

…only to find my fiancé backdooring a very large, very scary dude.

They hadn't realized I was there, so, feeling numb, I just stood and watched.

"Do you like that Bobo, do you? My big cock fucking your asshole?" Tiernan grunted out the words.

Bobo grunted louder in response.

Was I *really* standing there watching my guy bang *Bobo*?

Tiernan saw me out of the corner of his eye, and his dick just…popped right out. It was dripping with whatever lubricant he'd applied.

"Car, what are you doing here?"

"I'm getting a free show, Tier. What are you doing?"

"Oh, you know...just having a little fun...expanding my horizons and stuff," he said, his words mumbled. He glanced at his lover.

"Car, maybe you should cover yourself."

I realized Bobo was leering at me and quickly tied my coat closed.

"I'll leave you two to your...lovemaking." Then, realizing I wasn't being dramatic enough, I slung the duck blood soup at Tier. It exploded, covering both guys completely. Bobo had a piece of dried fruit stuck to his wrinkly, bald head.

The nude-dude version of *Carrie*.

"I'm outta' here."

"Wait, Caroline," Tiernan had to take a deep breath to get the next words out. "Please don't go. Let's talk about this."

"Not with that gorilla lingering. Tomorrow, Tier. Maybe." I walked out of the apartment.

***

I cried myself to sleep, but not before turning off my phone and engaging the chain lock on my front door. I wanted nothing to do with Tiernan Martin Diamond tonight...and maybe not ever again.

***

I awoke to a million texts from Tiernan, though they weren't the sappy, apologetic texts I expected. After I'd left last night, he'd had a panic attack and couldn't breathe. Bobo had rushed him to the emergency room, where they'd run a series of tests. Tiernan was perfectly healthy, yet the breathing problems persisted. They sent him home with some supplemental oxygen and appointments with a cardiologist and pulmonologist.

Feeling a little panicked myself, I texted back.

Caroline: Is Bobo still there?

Tiernan: No.

Caroline: Okay, I'll be over soon.

Tiernan: Please hurry.

Thirty minutes later I was back at the scene of the crime. Tier was lying on the couch, a nasal cannula plugged into a small canister giving him the oxygen his body required. He looked withered, as though he'd aged dramatically. A pulse oximeter, measuring his blood's oxygen saturation, sat on his finger, alarming every few seconds. I lifted his legs, sat on the opposite end of the couch, and placed them across my lap. He handed me the discharge papers from his ER visit. I looked them over.

"It seems like they did a pretty good work-up on you. Everything was negative. You're fine."

"Tell that to my body when I take the oxygen off."

I sighed. "Tier, I think it's psychosomatic. You're stressed that I found out you're not only cheating on me, but also, apparently, bisexual. I admit that would have been nice to know beforehand."

"I don't think that's it, Car. I feel really sick."

"Let's test it out." I removed the cannula from his nose. Within thirty seconds, his lips had turned blue, and he was gasping for air.

"Okay, maybe not psychosomatic, after all." I swallowed hard. "Yikes."

"What do you mean, 'yikes'?"

"I've worked as a nurse for years, and I've never seen lips turn cyanotic that quickly."

"What's cyanotic?"

"A blue discoloration caused by lack of oxygen."

"Great."

"Why'd you do it, Tier?"

He didn't have to ask what I meant. Still gasping a little from my experiment, he said, "I've always liked guys, Caroline. I just...wanted to keep it secret." He looked down. "Forever."

I let his words process.

"Are you telling me I'm your beard, Tiernan?"

He tried to sit up, but couldn't. He was too weak. He plopped back against the pillow and with zero fanfare responded, "Yes."

I took off my engagement ring.

"But I do care about you, Car..."

I leaped at him and tried jamming the gaudy fucking ring down his throat, but, realizing what was happening—that his fiancé had lost her ever-loving mind—he held his lips tightly closed, and they wouldn't budge. So, I did what any duped beard would do...I pinched the living shit out of his nose until his mouth was forced open to take a breath, and I stuffed that diamond down his lying, cheating gullet.

He began choking, grabbing his throat, begging with his eyes for compassion. For mercy.

I walked out of his apartment and shut the door.

"I'm the reason you *can't* breathe too, asshole."

The Academic Hearing Committee's Final Decision

By: Kenzie Jennings

The Academic Hearing Committee's chair, Dean Patrice Rogers (Academic Affairs), had switched off the Zoom meeting's record button in order for the committee to discuss their decision.

It would've been an easy one this time as the accounting student who'd filed the grievance had blatantly plagiarized his test answers from the class textbook.

A textbook that had been written by the professor who taught the class.

Unfortunately, the hearing derailed when one of the committee members, the infamous blowhard, Andon Metz (Business Ethics and Economics), was beaten to death, on camera, not so coincidentally with the textbook in question.

It had been one of those fine-but-certainly-not-fine situations, the sort of shocking moment that came with a side of apathy. Everyone else on the committee had wanted Andon to shut the hell up, and they certainly had their wish granted.

Andon had been about to play his usual, annoying game of either Let's Discuss the Ethics of Authorship or his favorite game of Devil's Advocate, which he always won, not because he was particularly clever at argumentation but because he wore everyone else out. When Dean Rogers had asked if there was anything else to discuss before the committee reached their decision (again, it had been in the bag), Andon had waited until just the right moment to interrupt the committee member, Gayle Atwater (English), who was primed to make a motion in favor of the professor's decision. He was about to go into one of his ponderous diatribes, in between loud slurps of whatever was actually in his coffee mug, when a figure dressed head-to-toe in black and wearing the all-too-familiar latex Melting Man mask came up from right behind his desk chair with the textbook raised and proceeded to whack the heavy tome hard against the back of his head, over and over and over again.

After the sixth hit, Andon's puffy face had smooshed flat against his screen, the force of the strikes shaking the image of Andon's already distorted facial features. At the tenth hit, his screen went dark.

Now academics have never been the kind—you know, the practical kind—to immediately take action and call 911. There were also no outbursts, no screams of horror, no fainting, no hysteria, none of that.

When Andon's screen went dead, for once in their tediously sluggish careers, no one said a damned thing.

That is, until Pete Jones (Sociology) broke the silence with a "We're not still recording, are we?"

***

Patrice Rogers
To: Peter Jones, Simone Haybert, Gayle Atwater, Jessica Roberts, Xavier North, Ryan

Price, Scott Franklin, Nicci Alana Davis, Alonzo Parsons, Dex Freeling, Krystal Rice-Johnson
    Cc: Candace Williams, Havland Hill

    Subject: Next   Academic   Hearing postponement

    Colleagues,

    Academic Affairs has heard each of your concerns regarding the February 5th incident involving the tragic demise of our beloved colleague, Dr. Andon Metz of the Business Department. We value your input, and we emphasize that your safety is of paramount concern. Due to this, our next Academic Hearing will be postponed until further notice.

    Over the next weeks, and as we've grown unfortunately acclimated to, we strongly advise you to refrain from contacting media outlets or answering any questions that may be asked of you about the incident in question or the "Melting Man." Per usual, direct all media inquiries to the Office of Public Affairs (ext. 2957).

    Regarding safety measures, Officer Jessie Lindover, our Chief of Campus Security, will be holding a two-hour briefing this Friday at 11:00 AM in the Warborough Auditorium. Until then, Officer Lindover advises faculty, administrators, and staff to be aware of their surroundings, even while at home, and make certain doors and windows are kept locked.

Attendance for the safety briefing is mandatory. Firehouse Subs will provide lunch.

If you have any questions or concerns, do not hesitate to reach out to the Office of Academic Affairs (ext. 2950).

Respectfully,

Patrice Rogers, PhD
Dean of Academic Affairs

Ryan Price
To: Gayle Atwater, Dex Freeling

Subject: ?!?!

Are either of you actually attending that sham of a briefing? If...*he*... wants us, he'll take us out anyway. If he was going to slaughter us all, we'd be dead, wouldn't we? At this point, we're four colleagues down, and zero from admin. Why is no one speaking honestly about any of this? Why is no one pointing out that admin isn't the group being targeted by this guy?

Gayle Atwater
To: Ryan Price, Dex Freeling

Subject: ?1?!

Sir, did you not get the memo that faculty are disposable? That whole "your safety is of paramount concern" is such a PR phrase. Don't want to rile the public servants. Pacify. Keep them calm. Remember it's not about them. It's about keeping students in the dark. It's about keeping the community from dropping support out of fear. It's never been about faculty. The selfishness, Prof. Price! I mean, really!

Ryan Price
To: Gayle Atwater, Dex Freeling

Subject: ?!?!

Can I say this here? Will IT archive this? You know what, I don't care. I'm going to say it. Melting Man...I think it's a student, one of ours. I think it's the one who had his mother there with him. You remember that one? He looked so embarrassed during the entire ordeal. Think he had some mommy issues. Let's take it one further. Norman Bates had mommy issues, didn't he? Are they going to cover *that* during the safety briefing?

My money's on "no."

While on the topic, what's a safety briefing going to do for us exactly? The entire state board is gunning for our jobs anyway. They won't have to think about a thing if we're all dead. So are you both going? Should we say something?

Dex Freeling
To: Ryan Price, Gayle Atwater

Subject: ?!?!

I don't know if I'm going. They're not even
willing to get us something other than Firehouse
Subs for lunch. I *know* we've a bigger budget to
afford ANYTHING other than Firehouse Subs.

Gayle Atwater
To: Dex Freeling, Ryan Price

Subject: ?!?!

Dex, no one cares about Firehouse Subs.
There are faculty being murdered.

Dex Freeling
To: Gayle Atwater, Ryan Price

Subject: ?!?!

I'm just saying I'm getting tired of the same
ol' same ol'. Olive Garden caters too, you know.

Ryan Price
To: Dex Freeling, Gayle Atwater

Subject: ?!?!

Really? Come to think of it, I think Outback does as well.

***

It wasn't easy for Dean Rogers to resume the next hearing, but life in academia goes on, and, emboldened by the actions of the Melting Man, students were making strong accusations against their professors more than ever before. Someone, after all, would likely murder that one professor who'd had it in for them since day one, citing and then hiding behind the safety of their syllabi policies, and that murder would be oh so glorious. It always was.

The first two hearings since the "February 5th incident" went on with nary a hitch, and it was enough to keep the faculty on the committee on their toes.

Until they weren't.

This time, Xavier North (Chemistry) was on the receiving end right when Dean Rogers had stopped recording so that the committee could discuss their decision.

The Melting Man lived up to his name when he clutched Xavier tightly against the chair and poured the liquid contents of a mason jar over Xavier's head.

It took approximately twenty, long, grueling minutes for Xavier to succumb to the damage done to his entire head, the acid having dissolved nearly all of the hair, skin, and meat from his skull. The acid was still working its way through the bone. By the time the committee members had gaped in horror at the scene unfolding in front of them onscreen, with a few of them still vomiting into various handy receptacles (although unable to get a trash bin in time, Krystal Rice-Johnson, Advising, had spewed all of her coffee and berry yogurt all over her screen), Xavier's remaining facial features consisted of nothing but a partial lower jawbone and a smoking flap of skin dangling from it.

"What do you want from us?" Dean Rogers said quietly into her camera.

The Melting Man reached over Xavier's shoulder and promptly shut off Xavier's feed from the Zoom meeting.

The committee members left simply sat there in silence, unable to do much of anything else. Simone Haybert (Registrar) had started to pray aloud. Ryan Price (Digital Media and Photography) spat out the remainder of the vomit that had coated the inside of his mouth right into his empty glass that had probably held his usual diet Dr. Pepper. Someone was softly keening, but it could've been any one of them.

Absolutely *any* one of them by then.

"Is our three-year commitment to this committee binding?" said Gayle, breaking the keening. "Because I'd like to recuse myself from it…forever."

Not one answered right away, the silence echoing in each of their rooms.

And then Dean Rogers said, "You only have a term left, Gayle. Wait it the hell out like the rest of us. We're up for accreditation review."

***

Gayle Atwater
To: Dex Freeling, Ryan Price

Subject: I hope the state archives this.

She's lost her damned mind. In fact, all of our admin. have collectively lost their minds. We cannot possibly treat any of this like it's the new normal. The parking lots are virtually empty every day now. I've had maybe 3-4 students in class, and they're only there because they have no place else to go. Everyone's terrified to leave their home, and everyone's terrified to *stay* at home. We can't teach anything effectively anymore, and they still expect us to attend meetings??

Did I tell you I bought a gun yesterday?

Ryan Price
To: Gayle Atwater, Dex Freeling

Subject: I hope the state archives this.

I've set motion-detecting cameras in and around the house now, and two of them are in my home office. If you two want to come over for the next meeting, we could use my office, attend together, or whatever one calls it. I've a feeling everyone else has the same idea.

Don't bring the gun though. Terri hates them, and what with the twins learning to walk now, not a good idea.

Gayle Atwater
To: Ryan Price, Dex Freeling

Subject: I hope the state archives this.

I'm not coming without some kind of weapon. I get why a group of us would be safer, but if we're not armed with something, at least one of us, we don't have a good chance of defending ourselves.

I can't believe I'm actually typing this, the fact that we're so focused on our safety during an *online* meeting and that I've even considered getting a gun, and you know how I've always felt about them. HOWEVER, these aren't normal times, Ryan. There is a serial killer targeting our committee members. A *serial killer*.

Better to be prepared because any one of us could easily be next. After all, we've always sided with the professor in every single academic hearing we've held. Not once have we been in favor of the student.

Ryan Price
To: Gayle Atwater Dex Freeling

Subject: I hope the state archives this.

That's because they CHEATED, Gayle, and there's evidence to support it. How else would we have favored anyone BUT the professor?

At any rate, if it's an angry, vengeful student, it wouldn't seem logical to target committee members who have the professor's evidence. Rather, wouldn't they target the professor in question?

So why us then? And why not any of the admin? or staff? What makes us so special?

Dex Freeling
To: Ryan Price, Gayle Atwater

Subject: Rate My Prof. Take a look!

My man, have you looked at your Rate My Prof. reviews lately? I took a look last night. You know how I am before the hangover hits. I do this every time.

Let me tell you, every one of us has had the same anonymous review (spelling errors and all): "I hold you ultimately responsible for my brother's unaliving." (Gayle, being the rhetoric specialist, I don't know if you already are familiar with this, but if not, it might interest you: They use "unaliving" instead of "suicide" these days on social media to avoid triggering anyone. I had no idea what this was.)

I did a little extra digging to save you the headache. Those of us on the committee are the only professors who have this particular rating. Granted, I didn't check the rating of every single professor at our college, but I had enough of a sampling to see for myself. Anyway, there's only one student who had committed suicide in the past twenty years. Back in 2011, a kid by the name of Roland Parsons who'd been taking classes, working part-time, and living out of his car, was found dead in a Denny's restroom stall, having slit his wrists. He'd left a letter to his little brother, Alonzo, on the sink counter.

I don't know what the letter said. There's nothing in the news archives about it. But I don't think it takes astute detective skills to see where this would wind up. It's got to be the brother. I'm going to be honest though, I don't remember that kid who'd died. Do either of you remember the guy?

Ryan Price
To: Dex Freeling, Gayle Atwater

Subject: Rate My Prof. Take a look!

I vaguely remember hearing about a student who'd killed himself around that time, but if he'd been in my class, he didn't make waves. He was about as insignificant as an adjunct. I don't mean to sound cold. I feel for the kid and his family, but that was over a decade ago.

The name sounds so familiar though. I know it from somewhere.

Gayle Atwater
To: Dex Freeling, Ryan Price

Subject: ON THE NEWS!

Rex, your timing is impeccable. Check your texts! I just texted both of you. It's all over the news. Alonzo Parsons has been arrested!

Ryan Price
To: Gayle Atwater, Dex Freeling

Subject: ON THE NEWS!

It's not Alonzo. They have the wrong guy. Unless he has some solid tech. skills, it can't possibly be him.

Gayle Atwater
To: Ryan Price, Dex Freeling

Subject: ON THE NEWS!

What are you talking about? Of course, he's the prime suspect. If he's the brother of the kid who killed himself, he has to be the one who'd posted those reviews!

Dex Freeling
To: Gayle Atwater, Ryan Price

Subject: ON THE NEWS!

Yeah, man, what are you talking about? Or writing about? (Whatever. This all seems counterproductive anyway.)

Ryan Price
To: Dex Freeling, Gayle Atwater

Subject: ON THE NEWS!

Friends, in case you weren't aware, and it seems like you weren't, Alonzo is our student SGA rep. on the committee. He was present at all of the meetings we've had. I've even double-checked the recordings in our archive. That kid was in the SGA office during each of them.

I knew I remembered the name from somewhere.

Dex Freeling
To: Ryan Price, Gayle Atwater

Subject: Zoom trickery

My man, you know you can change your background on Zoom in the settings, don't you? There are even backgrounds created just for us to look like we're in various places on campus...

…including the SGA office. ;)

Between that and learning how to enter grades in Canvas, you're on your way to joining the rest of us in the 21st century. How's that flip phone treatin' ya?

Case closed. That kid is done. Revenge is a nasty business. Too bad he got caught, eh?

Ryan Price
To: Dex Freeling, Gayle Atwater

Subject: Zoom trickery

Hey, I still know how to use an air fryer, my guy. Can you say the same?

On that note, you all are still welcome to join me at the house for the next meeting. We'll do brunch. Terri is taking the kids to the beach with a couple of her friends, so it'll be just us. I can whip up some omelets. Dex, you can bring the vodka. Gayle, whatever you want to bring, minus the gun.

We don't need that drama.

***

The next hearing was rocky but quick. The student in question had allegedly purchased her final paper for her philosophy class. She was a mess of tears and anger, sitting there in front of her laptop, insisting that she had written the paper, that whoever had written it had plagiarized it from her.

"The *audacity*," she'd said between sniffles.

Except the original date of the paper was April 7, 2002, and the student in question was eighteen years old.

As soon as Dean Rogers stopped recording, the committee had been ready, their decision swift and obvious. Just as Pete was about to make a motion in favor of the professor—

—and Gayle had snuck an extra pour of vodka into each bloody mary from beneath Ryan's laptop camera's view—

—two figures dressed all in black, the signature Melting Man masks hiding their faces, came in silently through the opened sliding glass doors of Ryan's lanai.

Before anyone in that Zoom meeting could say a word, before anyone could warn the trio of their impending doom, Gayle had swiveled around, her eyes widening at the sight of the intruders, her glass tipping and splattering its bloody contents onto the Persian carpet Ryan's wife, Terri, had picked up from her last trip abroad.

"But they caught you," she whispered, prompting Ryan and Dex to turn around. Gayle's brow furrowed when she realized there were two of them. "Both of you...? What? Why are there two of—?"

One of the Melting Men had promptly shut her up with a skewer through her eye and into her brain.

Ryan was instantly hushed too with a bullet to his head. The one holding the gun with the silencer then pushed Ryan's limp body from the chair and then plopped down in front of the laptop. Before Dex could get up from his chair, the Melting Man with the skewer had yanked the weapon from Gayle's head and gave Dex a warning rap over his own head with the skewer.

"Gentlemen, there's no need for this. There's no need for any of this," Dean Rogers said, her usually calm, steady voice wavering ever so slightly.

The Melting Man at the laptop removed the mask, revealing the rosy, grinning mug of a middle-aged woman with mousy wild curls and mischievous eyes. She clicked her tongue and shook her head at Dean Rogers, at the rest of the hearing committee who sat there, breathlessly waiting for her to speak.

The other Melting Man had removed their mask as well, and like the other, was a woman, dark-eyed and prim, a complete contrast to her partner. She kept the skewer trained on Dex who had held up his hands in surrender, his eyes flicking from the laptop to the bodies of his friends, to the front door.

"We're not gentlemen, as you can plainly see, Dean Rogers," the rosy-cheeked woman said to the camera.

"Who…who are you then? And what…what may we…what may *I* do for you?" asked the dean.

"We're part of the cleanup committee appointed by the President and Board. Our job is to rid the school of faculty who attempt to indoctrinate our students with unapproved, unacceptable curricula."

"But...but I've never even seen you around campus," sputtered Dex. "Do you even teach here? You've not been at any of our faculty meetings or—"

The rosy-cheeked woman barely stole a glance over her shoulder at Dex when she simply said in a mocking lilt, "We're just 'insignificant adjuncts.' You don't even know we're here now, do you?"

Before Dex could answer, the other woman stabbed him in the throat with the skewer, promptly cutting him off.

"Now..." The rosy-cheeked woman slid her chair closer to the screen. "Let's talk demands, shall we? You've a number of full-time positions open now, don't you?" Her grin spread wide. "And we have the board-approved curricula."

"Perfect," said the dean, clearing her throat. "In fact, I can do you one better. How about a tenured position, full benefits? Would that suffice?"

It was Pete who broke the silence on the faculty end.

"Since when was tenure an option here?"

END

Is That Voodoo Doll Anatomically Correct?

By: Robert Essig

You never think there's actually someone in your neighborhood who practices voodoo. At least Richard Johnson didn't see it coming. But people talk and rumors go around like VD at a desert rave.

Rumors were something Richard scoffed at, generally. But enough people talked about that Charlotte woman down on Acacia Avenue. The rumor was she'd pretty much screw anything with two legs and a beating heart. That had piqued Richard's interest, but the issue he was dealing with sort of nixed any wild fantasies he had about some aging nymph who had an open-door policy that should have been more of a warning than an invitation.

Richard's problem was that he couldn't get it up.

Like seriously dead down there. No movement. Nothing. And prematurely to boot! Richard was only thirty-seven. There should be no reason he couldn't get a rise out of his little soldier, but the thing just stopped working one day. He'd seen doctors, but they attributed it to early-onset erectile dysfunction. Their suggestion was the little blue pill, or some variation.

Or surgery.

And Richard wasn't about to have doctors cutting his member open, not with the risk of infection (which could cause the loss of his penis), permanent impotence (which was where he was at anyway), or a number of other terrifying side effects that was as bad if not worse than any given drug commercial on TV.

So, that all being said, Richard found himself in the home of Tracy Ysult, the neighborhood voodoo priestess, or some such thing. Turns out the rumors were true (which meant that good ol' Charlotte was probably just as horny as Richard had heard). He was beginning to believe in rumors.

Tracy didn't look the way Richard assumed she would. No bone in her hair, no Caribbean accent, no beaded doorways. It was kind of a letdown.

"So, you do voodoo?" Richard asked.

Tracy nodded. She had lazy eyes and a tired demeanor, as if being a voodoo priestess was the most taxing occupation on earth. "Yep. It's always been in the family. Who do you want dead?"

Taken aback, Richard said, "Whoa, let's take a step back here. I don't want anyone dead."

Tracy tilted her head. "Then what can I help you with?"

Suddenly Richard had stage fright. How was he supposed to tell this woman that he couldn't get it up? It was embarrassing. Shameful.

Tracy smiled. "Ah, I get it. You want someone to fall in love with you. Well, you came to the right place. That I can do just as easily as harming someone. Voodoo isn't just for harm; despite what Hollywood would have you believe. So, who is she? Do you have a picture?"

"I'm, uh, not performing the way I should be."

Again, a tilt of her head. "I'm not following."

"My little soldier hasn't been going to war lately."

"Still not following."

"I've got a wet noodle."

A shake of her head. "I'm afraid I don't understand."

"The fire in my loins has gone out."

"The fire in your—"

"I can't get it up!"

Tracy's eyes widened with understanding. "Oh, I see. Why didn't you just come out and say it? I can help you with that."

"You can?"

"Oh yes. I just need one thing from you."

"Anything!"

"A clipping of your hair."

Richard nodded enthusiastically, then looked down at his crotch. "A sample of . . . which hair?"

Tracy rolled her eyes. "The hair on your head."

"Which head?"

"Oh, for fuck's sake! I don't want your goddamned pubes. Give me a clipping of hair and come back in a few days. It'll cost you five hundred dollars cash."

"Five hundred?"

Tracy raised her eyebrows. "You're going to dicker with me when we're talking about your junk not working? I can put the flow back in your pipes, Richard. You can haggle all you want. I don't need your business. But tell me, how did those pills work, and how much are they? You'd have to buy them for the rest of your life. Do they work instantly? Because what I have to offer you works immediately. How about that surgery? I'm sure that will set you back five grand or more. And what about the side effects?"

Richard nodded. His expression was blank. How the hell did she know about the surgery? He hadn't even told her about that, or that the pills hadn't worked for him.

He used her scissors to clip a small tuft of hair.

##

Three days later Richard found himself back in Tracy's parlor. The place smelled of bacon. Not what he would have expected. He had to step over a baby doll and a pile of Legos on his way in. Also not something he expected out of a black magic woman.

Richard put the cash on the table and Tracy slid a small doll across to him.

"It's a voodoo doll," she explained.

Richard looked at the offering and almost laughed. It was very generic looking like pieces of burlap stitched together in the cookie-cutter form of a human and filled with stuffing. The eyes were stitched Xs, and the mouth stitched on with a blank expression. It did have a unique feature between its legs . . .

"Your hair is stitched into the head. That's what connects you to this doll."

"The thing's got a penis," Richard interjected.

"You noticed. It's a piece of pipe cleaner that I wrapped in pink thread. That right there is the solution to your problem."

Richard picked up the doll and examined it closer. He went to fiddle with the penis, but Tracy urged him against doing so.

"No no no, don't do that. Not unless you want to embarrass yourself in here."

"What do you mean?"

Tracy smiled. Upstairs there was a thump and the sound of young kids arguing. Tracy looked up, glaring, and then the arguing spontaneously settled down.

"As I was saying," she said, "let me tell you how it works. It's quite simple, really. You now have complete control over your, uh, your ED. Think of the doll as a switch. In the down position, you are, well, *flaccid*. But flick it up, and you will become, you know, shall we say, ready for action. Make sense?"

Richard nodded. "All the sense in the world."

"But be careful with the doll. I can't urge you enough on that point. Protect it. It functions like any voodoo doll. In the wrong hands, you could be in a world of pain."

Richard nodded; eyes focused on the knitted penis protruding from between the legs of the doll.

Tracy counted the cash as Richard thanked her and then left.

##

As soon as Richard got home, he pinched the little penis on the doll and flicked it up like a light switch, just to see what would happen. Immediately, he felt a stirring in his groin that he hadn't felt in years. In mere seconds he felt the tightness of an erection in his pants.

"Ho-ley shit! It worked."

He pulled down his pants and marveled at his erection. Solid as a rock. So hard the thing almost hurt! Unbelievable.

Richard had never believed in magic. He thought himself a rational man that believed in science over things like religion and mysticism. But these results couldn't be denied. This shit was the real deal.

It had been over a year since he'd been with a woman, and in that time he'd rarely been able to get it up enough to even pleasure himself, so this amazing feat of manhood had to be given a trial run. For science, of course. And—again, for science—he'd have to conduct the experiment several times for accurate data.

And yeah, it worked. Richard played a couple of rounds of pocket pool like no one's business. When he was finished, he grabbed the doll and gently depressed the pipe cleaner penis, which in turn caused his own erection to soften.

Richard slept well that night, dreaming of female acquisitions. He'd get back on Tinder and whatever other dating app was full of no strings attached sex fiends. It was so easy these days.

##

Or so Richard thought it was easy. Turns out not so much.

"What the fuck am I doing wrong?"

Richard had been trying to match with women for weeks, but nothing was coming of it. In the past, he'd match all the time, start talking through messages, and soon enough they'd meet up. Problem was, sometimes he couldn't *get* it up, and that would end things real quick.

After two weeks of working the dating apps, how was it, not one woman had matched with him? It was scientifically improbable. Richard changed his profile pic, his bio, his whole damn approach! He started looking for matches with threes, fours, and fives rather than his previous rule about no one less than a six, and still nothing.

At first, he was satisfied that he could at least flick the switch on the voodoo doll and rub one out at night after striking out on the apps, but he needed a woman. He yearned for warm flesh. For the moans of passion, eager touches, the wild, unadulterated sex that comes from random strangers who meet on the skuzzy avenues of the Internet.

Sitting on his bed, Richard grabbed the voodoo doll and used his finger to flick the little pipe cleaner penis up, instantly feeling the reaction on his own body. The routine of jerking it when all of his non-existent options were abolished was beginning to lose what little charm it had. The way Richard felt, he shouldn't have been able to get it up, and yet all he had to do was put that damn pipe cleaner penis in the up position and he was ready for anything.

##

As the weeks went on Richard began noticing a distinct phenomenon all around him. Whether he was at the gas station, at work, at the grocery store, anywhere, he was beginning to realize that women were repelled by him.

It was as if he smelled like a sewer, or had dog breath, or was cursed with horrendous acne, but none of those afflictions applied. Richard was clean, well-dressed, and handsome (well, he thought so).

Take the other day at Rigoberto's taco shop. All the seats were taken outside. A gorgeous woman ordered food, and when she picked up her order, there was nowhere to sit. Richard offered a spot at his table, but she cringed like he'd offered her a hit from a crack pipe. She sat at the next table with a guy smelling of malt liquor and cigarettes who couldn't keep food in his mouth while chewing like a fucking cow.

Little things like that were happening all the time. Not mere rejection, but repulsion, and Richard couldn't understand that.

Finally, things came to a crescendo. Richard never would have thought that he lived solely for sex, that was ridiculous, but as it turned out, taking his sexuality away was a massive blow to his ego, to his well-being. Getting that back was like getting the greatest gift. But what good was it when he was so detestable that no woman—not even a two or a three!—would talk to him, much less touch him?

At night he'd think about every moment in the day when a woman gave him that disgusted look. Sarah at the office didn't even make eye contact with him anymore, he caught Jeanette shudder as he walked by, and she had a face that had a serious aversion to mirrors. A random woman yelped out of nowhere when she caught sight of him. Another crossed herself. When was the last time Richard had seen someone cross themselves outside of some horror movie? What the actual fuck?

One evening Richard found himself driving through town aimlessly, thinking about what had happened to his life. Was he destined to be a no-dick loveless loser? Was the voodoo doll a bad idea? He had the doll with him. It was in the center console, the little pipe cleaner penis flicked up. As Richard trolled the streets, he had his zipper down, masturbating as he looked for hookers. He had no experience with prostitution. It was one of those things seen on TV and movies. He wasn't even sure he'd be able to recognize one if he saw her. But he knew that trolling the seedy side of town was a must.

Finally, he came across a woman who looked like the prostitutes he'd seen on episodes of COPS. She was scraggly looking, clearly on drugs, but wore short shorts, a skimpy top, and too much makeup. She was just sort of lingering there. Just like he'd seen on TV.

Pulling up to the woman, Richard said, "I'm looking for some fun."

Before she looked up at him, she said, "What kind of fu—" But then she made eye contact and the words died on her cracked lips. The cigarette fell from her mouth. She was frozen in fear.

Richard squinted. "What's the problem? Ain't my money as good as anyone else's?"

Her mouth opened and closed as if seeking the right words to get her out of this situation, but nothing came to her.

Grabbing his erection tighter, Richard's face reddened.

"What's your fucking problem?" he asked.

She remained glued to the sidewalk, stricken in fear.

Looking around, Richard saw that there was no one else out. He breathed heavily, squeezing his throbbing cock like he was trying to relieve stress. He opened the door and stepped out of the car. The woman saw the erection bobbing from the opening of his pants. She screamed and made to run, but he reached out and grabbed her with both hands. He flung her into his car, pushing her into the passenger seat, then he entered and closed the door, slamming the gear into drive and peeling out.

##

The following morning wasn't good at all.

I mean, is it ever good to wake up with a dead hooker in your bed?

Richard's recollections of last night were hazy. Not because he'd been drinking or something, but because he just didn't want to remember how far he allowed his desperation to get, how depraved he became. It was like he'd become someone else. He wasn't some kind of freak or pervert or anything. Of course, anyone who saw him driving around with a stick shift in one hand and his rod in the other might beg to differ.

The hooker was, well, not just dead, but bloody dead. Richard had even offered her money, but she'd been so sickened by him that she'd puked. That's what *really* sent Richard overboard. He'd seen the kind of guys who got a quick handy or BJ from working ladies. They weren't always the most hygienic fellows, at least not on shows like COPS. What was so disgusting about Richard?

After the puke, he'd lost it. Looking at her now, it was absurd to think that he could fuck the holes he'd put into her body, but he gave it his college best. The gut hole wasn't very satisfying. No traction, just squishy nothing. The slice to her thigh was actually kind of nice, but the muscle kept ripping. He'd cut her throat and tried cramming his cock down her esophagus, but that was more work than it was worth.

The most fucked up part of it all was that in the end he used her blood as lube and jerked off looking at her mutilated body.

Shame had consumed him immediately afterward. He violently pushed down the little pipe cleaner penis on his voodoo doll. Looking at the doll now, he could see black fingerprints of her blood on the thing.

Richard stood there before his bed, staring into the darkened blood and bluing flesh of a dead hooker, his own body marred by her dried blood, his cock and balls a crusty matted mess of gore that looked like it was covered in old chocolate pudding. He stood there and asked himself one question:

"How the hell did things get this out of hand?"

##

Richard pounded on Tracy's door. She opened it after a minute. On seeing him, she smiled a knowing smile.

Richard pushed his way into her house.

"What the fuck did you do to me?" he asked.

"You're not satisfied with the results?"

"Well, yeah, the doll works great, but something has changed. For some reason, women are grossed out by me. I mean, I'm not God's gift to the earth or anything, but I had game and now I . . . I can't even get a fucking hooker to let me *pay* her for sex."

Tracy smiled and nodded. "Then maybe you'd like one of my enchantments."

"I don't want anything from you. I just want you to take off whatever fucking curse you put on me to make women all hate me."

Tracy shrugged. "You're in charge of that. You see, the power of voodoo is sometimes more than even I can understand, but what I do understand is that sometimes voodoo has side effects, only I cannot rattle them off like in a TV commercial of Ambutrin or Fuckitol or whatever. I can say for certain 'may cause death' is one of the side effects of any voodoo magic."

Seething, Richard's breathing grew heavy. His heartbeat radiated through his body.

"But I can take care of your problem," Tracy said. "I have an enchantment that will lure all the women to you."

"No!" Richard stepped forward and then stopped himself. He was beginning to feel out of control again but was able to resist the urges. He was angry. Anger he could deal with.

"Better yet," Tracy said, "I can make it so that women are only attracted to you when you are using the doll. Believe me, if I put this enchantment on you otherwise, you'd be beating them off with a stick. Literally."

"I don't want any of your fucking enchantments or voodoo dolls or whatever. I just want my life back!"

She gave him a mock frown. "The no-dick life you came here to fix? The loveless life?"

Richard's face went blank. "You don't seem repulsed by me." He took a few steps closer.

Tracy's expression changed. The knowing smile faltered, her eyes widened just a little, just enough for Richard to detect the same disgust and fright he'd seen in every other woman's eye over the past month.

He shook his head. "You're just keeping your distance, that's it."

Tracy cleared her throat. "I can change this, you know."

Richard shook his head. He pulled the voodoo doll from his pocket.

"Yes," Tracy said, "hand me the doll and I can make an adjustment that will have any woman you want fawning over you."

Holding the doll in one hand, Rich used the other to bend the pipe cleaner penis into position, only this time pipe cleaner did what pipe cleaner always did after too much use. The little bendable metal snapped, and the pipe cleaner penis came off in Richard's fingers.

His eyes widened and his stomach dropped.

Tracy gasped. "Now you've done it!"

Blood seeped through Richard's pants, starting with a pinprick that swelled like ink from a leaking pen. He pulled off his pants and screamed when he saw that his penis had indeed fallen off. He grabbed it and held it out, scrutinizing the thing.

"What the fuck just happened," Richard said, his voice rising in panic.

As cool air hit the wound where his manhood had detached, searing pain sucked into his abdominal cavity and radiated outward through his entire body. He dropped his penis and collapsed onto the ground, clutching himself like a kid in dire need to go potty. Richard screamed.

"I can help," Tracy said.

"You fucking bitch! Look what you've done to me!"

"I didn't do this to you. You came to me for help. I helped. It was in your hands after that." She smiled that evil smile of hers. "Looks like it's really in your hands now."

Writhing on the floor, blood getting all over the place, Richard choked back screams, but the pain was horrendous. He sobbed and cried and figured if he died right here on her living room floor, at least she would be the one who had to deal with the consequences.

"Give me the doll," Tracy demanded.

Richard continued to sob and cry.

"Give me the fucking doll!"

He reached out his arm and handed off the now-bloody voodoo doll. He then looked around frantically, sifting fingers through bloody carpet. "The penis? Where's the penis?"

"Forget about it, Romeo," Tracy said as she examined the doll.

"But that's the most important part!"

"Maybe pipe cleaner was a bad choice of material for this application."

"Jesus it HURTS!"

Nodding, Tracy said, "I bet it does. Maybe I can help."

Richard looked up from the bloody mess on the ground, hope in his eyes.

Tracy took a deep breath. "Let me see, how does this work exactly? Ah yes, I think I can fix you up. It will be temporary, until we find something better than pipe cleaner."

She left the room. Richard writhed on the floor, whimpering in agony. He wondered if it had all been worth it. Had he known this would be the outcome he never would have agreed to this madness. He'd always heard that saying about thinking with the wrong head, and look what that got him.

Holding up his bloody penis like the skull in Hamlet, Richard said, "It's all your fault. Goddamn you."

"What are you rambling on about in here?" Tracy said as she reentered the room. She cringed. "For the love of all things good in the world, put that thing down. I have your fix right here."

She produced a small length of wooden dowel, broken at one end.

"Are you sure?" Richard asked. He was becoming pale from loss of blood.

Tracy brought the splintered end of the wooden dowel to the vortex of the voodoo doll's legs. She shook her head. "Nope. I'm not sure at all."

Tracy jammed the sharp end of the dowel into the doll where the little pipe cleaner penis had broken off. Richard screamed. Blood spewed from his mouth, erupting like red vomit.

"Oops," Tracy said. She pulled the dowel out and jammed it back into the doll.

Richard's body shook and trembled. The hole where his penis had fallen off became widened, blood and thick chunks of gore spilling out.

"No wait," Tracy said. "I'll get it right."

She continued to jam the dowel in, over and over until stuffing began falling out of the gash. Simultaneously, Richard suffered the same affliction, only his stuffing was red and wet with bluish-purple tangles and more red and more wet.

Tracy gave up as soon as she realized that Richard was dead. She tossed the doll onto the coffee table beside her copy of *Voodoo for Dummies* and sighed.

"One day I'll get a hang of this voodoo stuff," she said and then went in search of cleaning supplies to take care of the mess Richard made of her living room floor.

The End

Torture Porn for Prudes

By: Jeff Strand

"The delicious irony is that you've done absolutely nothing to deserve this," said Jamison, waving the hacksaw in front of his captive's face. "Your nightmarish fate was chosen completely at random. I could have taken anybody from that rest stop, and yet, it was...*you*. Makes you question the existence of a higher power, doesn't it?"

Fred struggled against the ropes that bound him to the chair in the basement. His voice was hoarse from screaming and he knew that pleading for his life would do no good. You couldn't reason with somebody who was pure evil.

"I'm going to do such horrible things to you," said Jamison. "I'm going to sever each of your fingers, cauterizing the wound after each one. Then I'm going to do the same with your toes. After that, I'll blindfold you and start making random cuts all over your body, but you'll never know where the next one will be! When you are bleeding from one hundred wounds—no more, no less—I shall remove the blindfold and very, very slowly slice off your nose."

Jamison smiled and winked.

"But your torment won't end there. Oh, goodness, no. I'll hold a mirror to your face, so you can gaze upon the disfigured freak that you have become. And then, out of mercy for how difficult it must be to see your new face so clearly,

I'll remove one of your eyes. Perhaps I'll make you eat it. Perhaps I won't. Why, I might eat it myself!"

Fred struggled again. But the ropes held firm. And he had nothing in his hands that he could secretly use to cut the ropes while Jamison was talking.

"And then, my undeserving victim, I will deliver the final misery. The final humiliation. The *coup de grace*. With this very saw..." Jamison waved the hacksaw in front of Fred's face again. "...I shall do the unthinkable. I shall cut off your ding-dong!"

"Excuse me?" asked Fred.

"I said, I shall do the unthinkable. I shall cut off your ding-dong."

"My...ding-dong?"

"Exactly!"

Fred snickered.

"How dare you laugh at me?" Jamison demanded.

"Sorry. I was terrified until you got to that last part."

"Do you not fear castration? What could be worse for a man than to have his ding-dong cut off with a hacksaw?"

Fred snickered again.

"What's wrong with you?" Jamison thought for a moment. "Are you in such a state of terror that you can do nothing but laugh at your plight? Is the laugh due to your lack of remaining sanity?"

"No, no, it's just...c'mon, *ding-dong?*"

"Don't pretend you don't know what a ding-dong is."

"I do. It's just not the word choice I would've expected from you."

"What's wrong with ding-dong?"

Fred giggled. "Okay, that's even funnier because it rhymed."

"Enough of your disrespect! You may be laughing now, but I assure you, you won't be laughing as the rusty blade of my hacksaw slowly slices deep into the tender yielding flesh of your doomed ding-dong!"

"Are you purposely trying to add comic relief?"

"No! This is serious business! I'm talking about inflicting ghastly torture upon you!"

"Okay."

"Stop smiling!" Jamison shouted.

"I'm not!"

"The corners of your lips are turned upward!"

"I guess I don't understand why you think I'd be intimidated by you calling it a ding-dong. What are you, six years old?"

"Fine! I shall do the unthinkable. I shall cut off your *wiener!*"

"My wiener?"

"Yes! Oh, I can hardly imagine your shrieks of agony as I draw this serrated blade back and forth across the skin and veins of your wiener!"

"That really isn't any better," said Fred.

"What's going on with you?" asked Jamison. "Did somebody already sever your wiener? Is that why you don't fear this mutilation? Is there no wiener available for me to remove?"

"Why don't you just call it a penis?"

The color drained from Jamison's face. "There's no call for that kind of language."

"It's not a curse word. That's what it's called. That's what a doctor would call it."

"I hardly think that a doctor is a good arbiter of morality."

"Ummm...okay. But I'd at least think a doctor would know the proper terminology. If you go in for a medical exam, the doctor isn't going to say, 'Let's take a look at your schlong.'"

"Enough!"

"What about phallus? Nobody can be offended by phallus."

"Phallus would make me sound pretentious," said Jamison. "You don't hear anybody say that word unless they're reading from a script. You'd think that I'd practiced my speech ahead of time instead of speaking from the heart."

"True."

"I honestly don't see the problem with ding-dong. It's not like I sang it."

"It's very juvenile. Took me completely out of the moment. Seriously, dude, I'm trying to help you out here. Call it a penis."

"I'll do no such thing! Mother would be horrified!"

"Then don't expect me to be frightened," said Fred. "You had a decent monologue going there, but you fumbled at the one-yard line."

"I don't know what that means," Jamison admitted.

"It's a football reference."

"If I was good at sports, I wouldn't have become a serial killer."

"Anyway, I'm not going to tell you how to do your job. I'm just saying—"

"It's not a job."

"Excuse me?"

"It's not a job," Jamison repeated. "Nobody is paying me to do this."

"Oh, sorry," said Fred. "My mistake."

"I will not be mistaken for some syphilitic whore doing vile things for spare change! I'm doing this for *me!* This is about *my* sadism! *My* uncontrollable urges! To suggest that I'm in it for a quick buck is incredibly offensive!"

"I already apologized. I don't know what more you want from me."

"I want you to die." Jamison sighed. "And now I don't even remember where I was going to start. You've gotten me completely flustered."

"You started out by saying that the delicious irony was that I didn't deserve this."

"Right, right, but I can't remember what I was going to do first."

"You were going to untie me, give me a ten-minute head start, and then try to hunt me for sport."

"Oh, you'd like that, wouldn't you? Now I remember. I was going to cut off all ten of your fingers."

"No, that wasn't it," said Fred.

"It most certainly was."

"I'm almost positive you said something about hunting humans being the ultimate adrenaline rush, but only when predator and prey were on even terms. You were going to give me a small knife to defend myself and then turn me loose."

Jamison slapped Fred across the face. "Enough of your lies!"

"Ow! What's your deal, dude?"

"I know what I said. I'm going to cut off your fingers, then toes, then the whole hundred cuts thing, then your nose, and then your eyeball. After that, to put it in terms that won't make you giggle, I'm going to take this hacksaw and use it to cut off your pe…your pe…" Jamison cleared his throat. "…your pee-pee."

"My pee-pee?"

"You know exactly what I'm talking about!"

"That's worse than ding-dong and wiener combined."

Jamison glared at Fred. "You deserve to die just for being so judgmental."

"That kind of messes up the whole idea that I haven't done anything to deserve this. You started your whole sinister monologue talking about how the delicious irony was that I was an innocent victim chosen at random. Now you're murdering somebody for being judgy. You've gone from making me question the existence of a higher power to just being petty."

"You know what's petty? Criticizing the word I use for your ding-dong!"

"Well, if you'd started off by threatening to cut off my dick, I would've been paralyzed with terror, and by now we'd already be on the third or fourth finger."

"And then Mother would have washed my mouth out with soap. Have you ever had your mouth washed out with soap? Have you?"

"No."

"It tastes terrible. Very bitter."

"Is it worse than having your dick cut off?"

"I couldn't say." Jamison raised an eyebrow. "Would you like me to wash your mouth out with soap first so that you can do a direct comparison?"

"Nah, I was just trying to be funny."

"Well, stop it. I'm not interested in being amused right now. This is not a lighthearted situation."

"It wasn't supposed to amuse you. It was supposed to make you angry. Y'know, so that you'd be filled with blind rage and make a mistake."

"What kind of mistake?"

"Shout in my face and get so close that I could bite your nose or something," said Fred. "I'm not sure why I thought that joke would enrage you. It was pretty mild."

"Are you ready to get started?"

"I guess I don't understand why you can't say penis and yet you're going to put your hand all over it later."

"I'm not going to put my hand all over it."

"You said you were."

"No, I said that I was going to saw it off."

"Right, but you have to hold it to saw it off. Otherwise, you won't be able to get any traction. It'll just flop around."

"What the heck are you talking about?" asked Jamison.

"Have you ever tried to slice a piece of bread without holding the loaf? It just moves around. To successfully cut off my putz, you'll have to hold it."

"So what? I'm not homophobic."

"It's not about homophobia. It's about having the proper maturity level to do the deed. Do you think a gay guy would be truly ready to do gay things if he said to his partner, 'Hey, I sure would like to interact with your ding-dong!'?"

"Look, I'm sure that in your normal life, you're all F-bomb this and F-bomb that and S-word this and S-word that and A-word, B-word, C-word, D-word, E-word all over the place. But I don't talk like that. There's nothing wrong with not having a potty-mouth."

"What's the E-word?" Fred asked.

"You know perfectly well what the E-word is."

"I really don't."

"It's when your ding-dong becomes aroused and engorged with blood."

"Erection?"

"You're disgusting."

"Maybe your prudishness is why you feel the need to kill. You're too repressed. Maybe if you just shouted the F-word a few times you'd let loose some of this pent-up frustration and live a happier life."

"I can't do that!" said Jamison. "Mother would hear!"

"What's she going to do to you? You're holding a hacksaw."

"Mother knows that I would never dismember her."

"C'mon," said Fred, "let it out. Say the F-word. You don't have to shout it. Just say it at a normal volume. You may find that you feel a lot better and aren't compelled to cut off my dick."

Jamison hesitated. "I can't."

"It's okay. I understand. Sometimes I'm a coward, too."

"I'm no coward."

"Oh, of course not. I take it bock, bock, bock."

"Did you just make a chicken pun at me?"

"I very well might have," said Fred.

"Do you really believe that calling me a chicken is going to change my...okay, fine, I'll say it." Jamison closed his eyes and took a deep breath. He opened his eyes again. "All right. Here goes. One...two...three...*fart!*"

"Fart?"

Jamison frantically glanced around, looking like he was in a state of panic.

The door to the basement opened.

"Oh, fudge," said Jamison. "Fudge, fudge, fudge."

The wooden stairs creaked as somebody walked downstairs. A short old woman came into view.

"What the fuck are you fuckers doing down here?" asked the woman.

"Nothing, Mother."

"Why the fuck haven't you chopped off his cock yet?"

"I'm getting to it, Mother."

"For fuck's sake, get this shit done, you lazy asshole!"

"Yes, Mother."

The old lady walked back up the stairs, shutting the basement door behind her.

"She's less prudish than I expected," said Fred.

"There's a bit of a double standard," Jamison admitted.

"But do you feel any better? Less psychopathic?"

"Not really."

"Well, fart." Fred began to struggle against the ropes again.

"Struggle all you want. Your fate is inevitable…"

* * *

The advantage to Fred having only one eye left was that it was more difficult to see his fingerless hands and toeless feet. The cauterization process had *sucked.* So had the one hundred cuts, especially the thirty-sixth and eighty-seventh ones. It was hard to breathe without a nose. And, in retrospect, it was naive of Fred to have thought that the eyeball removal would be no big deal. Watching Jamison eat it had been disgusting.

"And now it is time to cut off your ding-dong," said Jamison.

He began to use the saw. After a few tries, he grunted with frustration.

"You're right. It just keeps moving."

"I told you," said Fred.

"Fuck."

Also Available from St Rooster Books

From Tim Murr

The Gray Man
978-1799252177
Lose This Skin; Collected Short Works 1994-2011
978-1530351633
Conspiracy of Birds/Hounds of Doom
978-1516920631
City Long Suffering
978-1519588074
Motel on Fire; Stories
978-1543039016
Neon Sabbath; Stories

978-1721039708
My Skull is Full of Black Smoke; Stories
979-8680276099

Collection/Various Authors

To Be One with You; An Anthology of Parasitic Horror 2018 featuring Paul Kane, Marie O'Regan, Jeffery X Martin, Peter Oliver Wonder, Adam Millard, DJ Tyrer, David W Barbee, Ross Peterson
978-1724516787
Kids of the Black Hole; A Punksploitation Anthology featuring Sarah Miner, Chris Hallock, Paul Lubaczewski, and Jeremy Lowe

978-1072962724

The Blind Dead Ride Out of Hell; A Literary Tribute to the Amando de Ossorio Films featuring Sam Richard, Heather Drain, Paul Lubaczewski, Mark Zirbel, Jeremy Lowe, and Jerome Reuter

979-8692365187

A New Life by Paul Lubaczewski

979-8615384066

Blood & Mud by John Baltisberger

The God Provides by Thomas R Clark

979-8520227076

3 Hits from the Holler by Paul Lubaczewski

979-8707581984

Abhorrent Siren by John Baltisberger

978-1955745024

Let the World Drown: An Anthology of Sea Horror featuring Brian M Sammons, Lee Franklin, Jedediah Smith, AK McCarthy, Anthony S Buoni, BE Goose, Paul Lubaczewski, Jeremy Lowe, John Baltisberger, and Carter Johnson

979-8739852915

Souls in a Blender by Lamont A Turner

979-8494735201

Hungry Cosmos by Reed Alexander

979-8776862472

Black Friday: An Elder's Keep Collection by Jeffery X Martin

978-1955745093

Abhorrent Faith by John Baltisberger

978-1955745093

Short Stories About You by Jeffery X Martin

9798438145318

I Never Eat...Cheesesteak by Paul Lubaczewski

979-8440821415

Hunting Witches by Jeffery X Martin

979-8832793955

Saint's Blood by Ryan C Bradley

979-8804031863

As the Night Devours Us by Villimey Mist

979-8834327097

Parham's Field by Jeffery X Martin

SummerHome by Thomas R Clark

979-8838185136

The Ridge by Jeffery X Martin

979-8354516568

Through the Mist and the Madness: An Analytical Thesis on the First Three Metallica Albums by Jerome Reuter

979-8354143696

Like a Ton of Bricks by Paul Lubaczewski

979-8367912081

The Flock by Jeffery X Martin

979-8365780941

.

Printed in Great Britain
by Amazon